DARK NEW WORLD
- Book One -

JJ HOLDEN
&
HENRY GENE FOSTER

ISBN: 1530756383
ISBN-13: 978-1530756384

DARK NEW WORLD

- 1 -

0400 HOURS - ZERO DAY

CASSY SHORES SAT bolt upright in bed and knew that something was terribly wrong. Glancing around the hotel room, she felt a growing sense of dread as she realized it was pitch black. She paused to listen intently and then feel for anything out of the ordinary, but her other senses told her nothing.

Following a quick stretch, she slid off the bed, gingerly using her toe to find the floor. She felt around the little end table for the alarm clock, bigger than her cell phone and easier to find in the dark. It should have cast a red glow, but it too was dark. Turning it over, she checked every side, but it stayed stubbornly off. With a sigh, Cassy felt around for her cell phone and pressed the button to light it up to check the time. When it didn't activate, her heart began to beat faster.

Then she realized what was wrong: a city should have a quiet, ever-present hum of background noise, but there was only silence. She expected that kind of silence at her family's house in the middle of nowhere north of Lancaster, but it was utterly alien to urban Philadelphia.

Her mouth went dry and her heart pounded faster as she

crept to the sliding door that led to the room's tiny balcony and slid it open. Still there was no noise, no city hum. And no light—the city was as dark as it was quiet. She struggled to make sense of what she saw. Her brain was still sleep-fogged but was quickly coming back online with help from the colder night air outside.

The building abruptly quaked, and a deep, booming noise washed over Cassy. It echoed through the canyon of tall buildings surrounding her hotel. Her adrenaline surged, and she dove back through the open sliding glass door into her room, even before her mind registered the explosion. She laid face-down on the floor, clinging to it as though it could protect her if the building collapsed, while her mind caught up to what had happened.

Looking through the windows and door, she saw a fierce red glow reflecting off the glass of the building across the street. The light replaced the darkness of night and then slowly faded out until all was again black. Cassy waited for what seemed hours, but was probably only moments, and then climbed to her feet while running shaking fingers through her tousled hair.

A loud pounding on her door made her jump. Cassy carefully made her way through the darkness to the door and opened it. The hallway beyond was also pitch-black and she saw no one at first, but then she heard a baritone voice.

"Cassy, are you alright?" asked the voice, which she recognized. It was Tyrel Alexander, a co-worker who was also at the hotel in preparation for the next day's conference.

Relief flooded through her. "Yeah, thanks, Ty. What the hell was that?"

"I don't know. I can't see a damn thing. But I figured I'd make sure you were alright before going out to look. Want to come?"

"Sure," she replied. "Let me get some clothes on.

Whatever it was, it was loud and bright. Come on in."

"Yeah, scared me. Knocked out the power, too, it seems. I'll be right here by the door, girl."

As Tyrel waited for her to dress, Cassy couldn't see him but felt reassured by the rustle his clothes made each time he fidgeted. She didn't bother being shy—she couldn't safely find the bathroom or her suitcase in the blackness, and he couldn't see her just then anyway. She slipped off her robe in the dark and put on the dress she'd worn the night before, which was still by the bed. She put on her furry moccasin slippers and cautiously inched towards the door.

"Okay, let's go," she said and felt around until she made contact with his jacket. "I don't want to get separated, so I'm hanging on to you. Do you know the way?"

"Yeah," Tyrel said. "The stairwell is two doors down, I remember. Funny, I'd think the emergency exit lights would be on, right? They're on batteries."

"Let's just go. If we can get to the lobby, we can look around. Maybe a car bomb went off or something. But the lights were out before the building shook."

Tyrel grunted in response, and they kept moving.

The two crept along the hallway, fingers on the wall for guidance, until they found the second door. It took a long time to descend the stairs in the dark, but they made it to the lobby level and emerged from the stairwell. Here too everything was dark, but there was more noise as several other people called out, asking questions to which no one had any answers.

"Let's look outside," said Tyrel, and Cassy grunted in agreement.

They made their way to the huge glass double-doors of the hotel and stepped outside with caution. Cassy could see a little by the light of the waning moon, but not far. She saw no headlights, no cars moving. There were only a few people outside at whatever time of the pre-dawn morning it was, and they seemed to be doing what Cassy was doing— standing around just looking.

"My car is real close to the front doors," Cassy finally said. "I have a flashlight in the glovebox."

It was Tyrel's turn to follow Cassy, and they made their way to the nearby parking lot. "Third car from the street," Cassy said.

Once she got the car unlocked it only took a few seconds for her to find the rugged metal flashlight. Clicking it on, she turned in a circle slowly, using the beam to light up her surroundings, but saw nothing interesting. She slid into the driver's seat and put the key in. When she turned the key, nothing happened. She tried again, but still nothing.

Cassy sat motionless for a minute, thinking. "How's your phone, Tyrel?" she said.

"My battery died."

"That's what I thought about my phone, too. So, the lights are out, the phones are dead, and the cars aren't running."

Tyrel frowned. "But it's just a blackout, right?"

"Maybe. But if it was just the power grid down, why won't the cars start? And the cell phones aren't working at all, not even powering on."

"Bullshit, Cassy. You make it sound like aliens killed electricity or something."

"No, not aliens. But something has brought down all the electrical devices, and the power grid. You understand what I'm saying?"

Tyrel paused for a long moment before replying. "I'm going back to my room to go to sleep. It's still crazy early, feel me?"

Cassy nodded. "Yeah. Listen, at first light, I'm going to figure out what to do. Be at my room then, if you want to come with me." Voice dripping with friendly sarcasm, she continued, "If not, good luck and I'm sure I'll see you at work Monday."

"Yeah, I'll see you Monday. I'm going to stay in my warm room until they get the lights back on. I'm sure not going to that stupid conference tomorrow if the power is still out. Extra day off, yay."

Cassy let out a forced laugh and then she and Tyrel made their way back up to the fifth floor of the hotel.

She slid into her room and locked the door, and then carefully moved to the bed. Sitting down, she pulled out her cell phone and tried again to turn it on, without success. "By God," she muttered, "don't let this be what I think it is."

Deep inside, though, she knew. She'd prepared for this day, but facing the reality of a total grid-down situation made her hands shake and her knees weak. A more terrifying thought struck her—what of her children? They were with Grandma Mandy, Cassy's mom. But as much as she loved her mother, Cassy knew how poorly prepared her mom was for an emergency of any kind, much less a total grid failure.

Cassy sat on her bed numbly wondering what to do. She felt as though her thoughts were moving through mud, due to the shock. "Okay, Cassandra, stop. Think. What are your options?"

She tallied them off in her head and felt much clearer now that she had something solid to think about. The first decision was whether to stay in the hotel or leave it. If she stayed, she was betting that someone could get the system running again within a couple of days. After that, the stores would be empty and the Philly natives would be hungry and restless. If that bet paid off, everything would be fine, but if it didn't, well... She shuddered to think what the city of a million and a half people would be like in a few days without food. And, she thought, the odds of getting everything back up and running soon were frighteningly small.

Or she could leave the hotel, but she only had two places to go—her mother's house or her own. She wondered whether her mother would think to leave her house early enough. No, she knew her mother would wait until it was too late before realizing the hope fairy wasn't going to fix this. At her mother's age, and given the age of her own children who were with Grandma Mandy, it was best they stayed put unless they left immediately. Grandma couldn't make the trip on her own, most likely.

Cassy sighed in resignation. Her mother had teased her when she had started preparing for disasters, but Cassy had always just told her it was better to have it and not need it. Although, if she was honest with herself, she wasn't as prepared as she could have been. The recession had made everyone's lives tougher, and she had to tighten her own belt as well when her employer started pay cuts and furlough days. Still, she had a generator and other supplies, and enough food to feed everyone in her family for at least a year. If they could all just get to Cassy's house intact, everything would surely be fine.

But first she had to get them there, on foot, amidst the madness that she knew would soon come when the stores were bare.

- 2 -

STAFF SGT. TAGGART sat with three other soldiers in an ancient HMMWV, watching the landscape creeping by.

"Hey, Sarge. What's with this Charlie Foxtrot?" asked the soldier next to him. To SSgt Taggart, he looked young enough to still be in school.

"Do you mean, why were we ordered to leave our cozy barracks at Fort Doom at zero-dark-thirty? In the oldest Humvees in the lot? Scattering towards New York, every unit via a different route? The answer to all those questions is the same. Because we're ordered to."

"Yeah, but why are all the POVs on the road dead?"

"God hates civilian vehicles, numbnuts. Now shut your mouth and open your eyeballs."

Taggart had, of course, been wondering the same thing. Everything had died just as they had the gear stowed and were getting ready to head out. Cell phones, cars, lights. Everything but these ancient HMMWVs, which the grease monkeys had for some reason been working on days before the orders came to move out. Taggart wondered how far things had gone and why they had orders to split up and get to New York City. The rest of the soldiers in his unit would arrive in New York on foot, almost two weeks after his own unit arrived. The jarheads from the Iron Horse Marines had left a few hours earlier, with about half their vehicles. He presumed their other vehicles were dead, like most of his own unit's vehicles, and like these cars all over the road.

From the driver, he heard a snarl. "Goddamn, more POVs, Sarge."

Taggart felt immediate irritation and clenched his fist. There had been few cars on the road at first, but as they approached Gettysburg it had grown worse. Approaching York, there were enough dead cars to block the roadway. He looked out the window and saw that the blockage was on a small bridge between the remote York Airport and the city proper.

It took twenty minutes to get everyone turned around. They backtracked to the nearest turnabout and then continued north going the wrong way. He decided not to ask the CO of his little group why they hadn't done so an hour ago. Soon enough it wouldn't matter—a bit farther was York itself, which was almost guaranteed to be full of dead cars. Eventually, they'd have to stop and move some, slowing them down to a crawl.

The miles strolled by and Taggart saw that the road into York was another Charlie Foxtrot, a clusterfuck of cars blocking the roadway. He checked his watch, a windup that still worked: 0815 hours. It had taken them four hours to get this far. In normal circumstances, it would take only an hour more to get from Fort Doom all the way to New York City.

Taggart calmed himself and prepared his mind for the long haul. After York would be more frustration, mile upon mile of road with a dozen little bridges to get stuck at, and the huge one at Susquehanna River. They would hit gridlock in Lancaster before they could get off US-30 and onto I-76.

"Alright apes, get out and clear these cars," barked Taggart, and filed out with his soldiers to make sure they did so efficiently. He tasked a few soldiers to stand guard though it didn't seem necessary. Still, Taggart took no chances.

The slow going got even slower when the civilians who stayed in their cars protested being moved—they thought rescue had arrived—and complained when soldiers roughly pushed their cars out of one lane to clear it. They demanded answers, and transportation. They begged for help, any kind of help. When the soldiers ignored them they complained louder but, warier now, didn't approach. That satisfied Taggart—his boys carried live ammo today, and he wanted no civilian casualties if he could avoid them.

In a half hour, it was clear, and the soldiers rolled out, passing the cluster of roughly thirty people who had gathered. Of course, they wanted a ride, but there wasn't room to take them all, nor did Taggart's orders include slowing down to caravan civilians.

The small convoy rolled out with Taggart looking somberly at the frightened civilians they left behind, wondering if events would prove they were luckier than the soldiers.

- **3** -

AMANDA BLAKE WOKE to the sounds of her grandkids complaining. It was bright outside, the sunlight streaming through the curtains in her room, and she covered her eyes until they adjusted a bit.

"Grandma Mandy," came the chorus of outraged cries from the living room, and Mandy grumbled as she looked for her slippers. She straightened her nightgown and glanced at the alarm clock, wondering if it was time for school yet, but the clock was dead. She looked at her watch, a beautiful self-winding piece her late husband had given her when Cassy was born. It was a quarter after eight.

"Why didn't you wake me up, kids? You have school, and you know it takes a half-hour to get there from here. Lord bless you kids, but you'll be late now," she muttered to herself.

Grandma Mandy, as the kids called her, was still uncoordinated from sleep. When she opened her bedroom door, she almost stumbled. "God bless it," she said in frustration.

Aidan, the younger grandchild, said, "Careful, Grandma.

If you break a hip, we can't go to school."

Aidan was only seven but had a twisted sense of humor already. This often irritated his grandmother, but just as often delighted her. She blamed his humor on his mother, letting him watch zombie shows and all those end-of-the-world disaster movies.

"True, kiddo. But then I also couldn't make you breakfast," Mandy said with a grin. "So, why didn't you kids wake me up when the bus came?"

"Well, obviously because it never came, Grandma," replied Brianna, her oldest granddaughter, with a dramatic roll of her eyes. She was thirteen and tomboyish, still, and beginning to suffer the swinging moods of adolescence.

"Oh, a hooky day, then. If your mom agrees, I'll take y'all fishing, okay?" asked Mandy.

Aidan's eyes went wide with excitement as Mandy grabbed her cell phone off the counter, where she left it each night. But as she tried to turn it on, she cursed under her breath. "I hate these things. I can never get them to work right."

Aidan said, "Well, Brianna's phone doesn't work either. She couldn't tweet to her boyfriend this morning."

Brianna ignored Aidan's comments. "Grandma, the TV won't work and the lights are out, too. It's a blackout."

"That doesn't make sense. Why are the phones out, too? This is weird. Okay, kids, get dressed. We're going fishing until the power comes back on."

Twenty minutes later they were all dressed and ready. They carried bundles of fishing gear and plastic chairs to the door. Mandy opened it and let the kids out first, but realized she had forgotten her keys. She called out to the kids to wait for her and then went to find them. When she came outside with the keys, the first thing she saw was Aidan and Brianna standing stock still, staring at something.

She turned her head to see what they were looking at and then froze. All up and down her quiet street, people stood around their cars or sat in them. Others had the hoods up. But they all had one thing in common: none of the vehicles were running.

"Oh, my God," whispered Brianna.

Mandy shook herself free of her shock. The kids needed her to be calm, she told herself.

"What the fu—" Aidan started to say, but Brianna cut him off with a smack on the back of his head.

"Grandma will kill you dead if you say that word, little boy," Brianna told him sternly.

"Calm down, kids," said Mandy with as much cheer as she could muster. "I'm going to try my car."

She got into the brown Lincoln in her driveway and tried the key. Nothing.

When she got out of the car, Aidan ran up to her and wrapped his arms around her.

"How is mom going to come get us? What if *all the cars* broke?"

Before she could reply, there was a tremendous noise of shattering glass at the neighbor's house, and Mandy reflexively covered Aidan with her body as her head spun towards the noise.

"Goddamn truck," her neighbor Frank Malters shouted as he stood facing his F-150, fists on his hips. A tire iron protruded from the ruined windshield.

Mandy started to push Aidan towards the house. "Come on, kids, go inside. Nothing to see here, but we'll have to drive to the lake another time."

The children didn't argue with her this time, and Mandy saw they were becoming more frightened. Neighbor Frank's tantrum hadn't helped the situation, either.

With the kids playing Go Fish, Mandy calmly walked

around to ensure every door and window was closed and locked tight. Then she went to the refrigerator and looked inside. All that damn food would go bad if the power stayed off. The stuff in the freezer should be fine for a few days, but anything in the fridge had to get used up or tossed out that night.

But would the power still be off? Probably, she admitted to herself. The only thing she could think of that would kill cell phones, cars, and the power lines was a solar flare. At least, that's what had done so in some sci-fi disaster movie her daughter had made her watch with Aidan "so he wouldn't get scared." Of course, Aidan wasn't the one who got frightened.

She chuckled at the memory, but then stopped—what if the power *stayed* off? Would she ever be able to watch a movie with Aidan again? If the power did stay off, there was no way they could stay where they were for more than a few days. She had maybe a week of canned or dried foods: Campbell's Soup and spaghetti, mostly. Her neighborhood was full of well-off retired folks and upwardly mobile couples with few or no children yet, so no help there. Food would be scarce for the neighbors, as well. The nearest convenience store was ten blocks away, and the closest supermarket was more like twenty minutes by car.

Yet, her daughter Cassy's house was fifty miles away near Lancaster. It had lots of food, she knew vaguely, because her daughter was one of those crazy types that prepared for disasters of all sorts. Maybe not so crazy, she admitted. Still, it would be unsafe for a fifty-five-year-old woman and two children to travel so far, alone and on foot. And, she decided, Cassy would come for them, and would get them all safely to her own house. If not for Mandy herself, then definitely for the children—Cassy would never leave Aidan and Brianna behind, she knew.

Mandy pulled her "memory box" out from under the bed, a small cedar chest containing all her late husband's photos and his most cherished things.

"Bert, I wish you were here," she said sadly as she looked into the box of memories. She spared a moment to remember the times she had with him and fought back tears. But then she pulled herself together, and took from the box a small .38 revolver, handling it with obvious caution and distaste. She put it into her clutch bag, and then went out to play Go Fish with her grandkids.

"So, we're all going to stay inside for a while until your mom comes to get you," she announced, then sat down and began dealing cards.

- 4 -

0800 HOURS - ZERO DAY

BY THE LIGHT of day, Cassy looked at the two bags she had brought on this road trip to Philly, which were neatly placed on the bed. One was a suitcase containing clothes appropriate for a conference, or for after-hours business dinners. The other contained a set of rugged clothes, hiking boots, and a smaller backpack with many pouches and zippers. She pulled out the backpack and opened it, checking the inventory again even though she had already checked it right before leaving the house.

Some water, an MRE, a tarp, paracord, a Mora knife, a small .38 revolver, and two speed-loaders. She had 18 rounds, total. She used to have a larger pistol in her "get home bag," but with the water, weight was an issue.

There was also a small sealed tin with cotton balls soaked in Vaseline for starting fires, a bic lighter, and a little first-aid kit. A spare pair of socks and three cotton bandanas. The flashlight worked. Rounding out her little collection was a second tin that contained a wire saw, safety pins, fish hooks and so on, and it was neatly sealed with duct tape strips. Everything was in order.

Cassy looked in the mirror. At thirty-three, she was not gorgeous but knew she was 'very cute and nicely curvy', as most people described her. She was 5' 6", fairly fit, with shoulder-length brunette hair that was almost always in a ponytail. The "little black dress" she had on was totally impractical, so she stripped down and then put on her rugged clothes—loose-fitting brown canvas pants, thick socks, a black tee shirt, a blue flannel, a zip-up hoodie, and a heavier jacket.

But then she felt hot. She knew she had a long way to go, so she reluctantly left the heavier jacket on the bed. She had another jacket at home, but would never get there on foot if she passed out from heat in the still-warm August daytime weather. She put on the backpack and, with a glance at all the things she was leaving behind, left the room.

She went to Tyrel's room and pounded on it. When he answered, she saw that he could barely stand straight, and his eyes were bloodshot. Tyrel was of average height, but slightly plump from drinking more than he should. He kept his hair in neat cornrows, usually, but this morning even those looked disheveled.

"Hey, Casshy," Tyrel said, slurring his words.

Cassy felt pity for the man. He would likely die here, she thought, because he wouldn't take this seriously until it was too late. Like so many others. "Hey, Ty—I'm heading out on foot. Want to come with me? I could use the company."

Ty tipped sideways into the wall, but with effort maintained his balance. Somewhat. "Ouch. Nah. Why leave? Wanna have a drink with me til the power'sh back on?"

Cassy looked at him for a long moment, memorizing his face one last time. She doubted she would see him again in this lifetime if her suspicions were correct about what was about to happen around them, and decided she would miss his constant attempts to flirt with her. This would be goodbye. "No thanks, I'm heading out. Take care, my friend. Go round up some food and keep it in your room, okay?"

Cassy turned and walked away without another word, fighting back tears.

A quick trip down the stairs took her to the ornate lobby of the hotel. It was a 4-star joint, for sure, with great imported rugs and middle-grade art on all the walls. Soon it would be empty of people, she realized with a start, but for now, it was somewhat full of other people milling around. She knew some of them, and the sadness grew, so she decided to slip out unnoticed. That was easier than saying goodbye, and most of them would probably be dead soon. Back straight, she walked out through the ornate doors and onto the streets of Philadelphia.

Cassy gasped at the scene before her. Thick, acrid, black smoke billowed into the air from a couple blocks away, and dozens of people were making their way towards the source of that smoke. She walked in that direction as well, because it was the shortest path to where she needed to go. As she got closer, the knot of fear in her stomach, which had been there since she woke in the dark, grew steadily. Ahead of her, it became evident that buildings had collapsed, and she thought that must have been the cause of the overwhelming blast that had hit while she was on her balcony. She hadn't seen it then because her room faced away from the terrible scene. Two buildings were rubble, and two more were burning. People jumped out of upper windows rather than burn alive, and then Cassy did cry.

From bits of overheard conversation, as she hurried past the scene, she learned that a passenger jet had crashed. Some said another had crashed as well, to the east. "Just fell out of the sky. Good thing it was so early, or more planes would have been up there to hijack," said a middle-aged office worker to a man in a suit as Cassy walked by. By the time she got past the devastation, real fear gripped her heart and she mourned the hundreds of people in those falling planes, though she didn't know them. She felt the tragedy of it all and knew more terrible things were on the way.

She considered joining the rescue effort going on, led by everyday people stepping up in terrible circumstances, but she had different responsibilities. She had to get to her kids while she still could. Cassy continued on, heading north towards the city limits. It was miles away, but if she could clear Philly before the panic and looting began in earnest, she had a good chance. "Get ahead of the mob," she muttered.

She saw more people at every store she passed. There was a fight over the last can of something, but Cassy didn't stay to watch. She avoided the crowds of people stripping the stores bare by getting onto the next onramp onto I-76, which cut the city in half north-to-south, and the going was easier. She didn't see any people in the jammed-up dead cars; they must have already left in the hours since the blackout began. Somewhere far behind, she heard two popping noises; someone was shooting back there. She hadn't thought violence would begin so quickly when she was considering various "prepper scenarios," but at least those were the only shots she heard so far.

* * *

Cassy looked off into the distance to the west and north, the way she had to go. Suburban sprawl lay as far as she could see, and a sense of despair came over her.

"Shit. How will I get through all that?" she cried out and realized she had spoken aloud. She stopped to clear her head, taking deep breaths until her anger and hopelessness had lessened. She then looked around with more care. The freeway she was on was not completely clear, but there weren't as many people as there were on the streets below. Also, the freeway had concrete barriers running along both sides and down the middle. If she stayed close to the barriers dividing the two halves of the freeway, perhaps people who were off the roadway wouldn't see her, and the middle divider would give her some protection from everyone else. Not for the first time, she wished she'd been able to take a class on search and evasion techniques, but money was short since her husband died and the Great Recession had hit.

Cassy thought it over out loud. "So, fewer people and good cover, or more people to blend in with, but more possible threats and less cover." She decided to stay with more cover on the Interstate.

By noon, she had almost reached the outskirts of the city, and only then did she relax a little. Urban sprawl still lay to the west, but the north showed more trees than buildings. She walked onward and prayed the freeway was the right choice.

An hour later, Philadelphia was behind her. She stopped to take a drink of water and a couple bites of the so-called "fruitcake" that came in her one MRE. The fruitcake was terrible and tough as leather, but packed with carbs and calories and could be just gnawed upon while traveling. She was hungry but had to make the MRE last.

Also, she needed to rest her legs. By Cassy's calculations, based on her pace count—she knew how many steps it took her to go one hundred yards on level ground—she had walked roughly twelve miles in about five hours, and she was exhausted. What was supposed to be a short water break got longer and longer—her legs had cramped up and felt like rubber, and her new rugged hiking boots had given her one hell of a cluster of blisters. Goddamn new shoes, she should have broken them in *before* she needed them... Lesson learned.

Five hours to travel twelve miles was nothing to an athlete, but Cassy was in her early thirties and spent more time commuting to meetings than she did on physical conditioning. She was rather glad she had taken to gardening and raising animals at her home north of Lancaster, giving her some regular physical activity. A year before that, she had been in even worse physical shape.

She tried standing, but her legs just wouldn't obey, so instead she sat and massaged the muscles, resting. Maybe she should camp out here for the night despite having plenty of daylight left, she considered. She had a long way to go and it would take longer if she hurt herself overdoing things. Her thoughts drifted off to her children, and what horrors the future might hold for them all.

- 5 -

1430 HOURS - ZERO DAY

THE RUMBLE OF an engine echoed along the freeway. Cassy opened her eyes and was disoriented. The sun was definitely not where it had been, and she realized she had fallen asleep. What an idiot, she thought, realizing she was out in the open. She looked around for the source of the noise and saw an old red classic Camaro coming up fast. Before she had time to consider her options, it swerved and began to slow. Whoever was inside had seen her, and now it was too late to go for the pistol in her get-home bag, without being seen doing it. She could only hope the driver was friendly.

The Camaro glided to a stop some twenty feet from Cassy and then did nothing for nearly a minute. She couldn't see through the thick tinting of the windshield to see the driver, but the car was a thing of beauty. Perfectly maintained. "Cherry."

Cassy inched her way towards the center divider, ready to leap over the concrete wall if necessary, but then what? Her bag was out of reach, and if she went for it the car's occupant—or occupants—might react aggressively. She didn't know what to do, so she stood still and waited, alert.

The driver's door opened. Out stepped a man of average height, but muscled. Not like a bodybuilder, but he definitely worked out or worked hard. He had close-cropped black hair and a short goatee, and wore simple jeans and a white tee shirt, with black boots. His face was sharp and angular, and he might have been Italian or Puerto Rican, or just well-tanned.

"So, um..." began the man. "Well, I'm driving the way you're walking, if you want a lift. I'm James. Friends call me Jim."

"Hey. I'm Cassandra," she replied. "How can your car be running?"

The man laughed, and Cassy thought he sounded good-natured. "It's old—no electronics. Everything with a chip is busted, right? But no chips in this old beauty."

"Huh. Old-school muscle still works," said Cassy. "So, what brings you out of Philly?"

"Well, shit's already getting crazy in there. It's been about twelve hours since the lights went out, and the stores are already mostly empty. Idiots are barbecuing in the streets, thinking this is just a day off work. Try telling them a simple blackout doesn't kill cellphones and cars, and they look at you like you're an idiot or a conspiracy nut."

"So, where are you headed?" Cassy asked.

"Back home. My house is in the town of King of Prussia, maybe ten miles from here along the 76. If you want a ride, I can take you that far. Get you away from the nuthouse Philly is becoming. Besides, it's a nice day for a drive, right, honey?"

Cassy had to think about his offer. Who knew how fast the crazies would come off their leashes with the grid down, and was this guy one of them? Until the grid was back up she wouldn't be able to call 911 if things went sour, nor were the police just driving around patrolling anymore. If this guy turned bad, she'd surely be on her own. Cassy saw that he wasn't dressed as well as most people she'd met from King of Prussia, but his car probably had cost so much to refurbish that he *could* be a resident of that well-off town.

But she was exhausted and her legs were still rubber, so she desperately wanted that ride. Something didn't quite feel right, said an itch of warning in the back of her mind, but Cassy dismissed the feeling and chalked it up to exhaustion and panic, and from having watched too many horror movies. After all, he did seem nice enough.

"Yeah, alright, as long as you're going that way anyway I'd love a ride. Thanks a bunch, Jim. You're alright."

Cassy grabbed her bag and got in, and they drove off. The going was slow because of all the dead cars on the road, but, fortunately, most were on the other side of the freeway having been driven towards Philadelphia. The only people they saw were on the other side, too, walking towards the city. Even so, they had to stop several times to move cars out of the way, and at one point an overturned semi blocked the road. They had no way to move it, so they had backtracked to a turnabout and continued on the other side of the road for a while until they reached the next turnabout.

It had taken them about an hour to go five miles, but at least she was off her feet except to help move cars out of the way. Exhausted, she found herself drifting to sleep on an open stretch.

She came to full alertness when the car stopped and went silent. Opening her eyes, she looked around and saw no cars, yet they were stopped in the middle of the road, engine off. She looked at James with concern. "What's going on, more cars to move?"

"Nope, I'm out of gas. I have to grab my gas can and go siphon some off one of those cars back there, but it's about four o'clock and I don't want to get caught out here in the dark. No street lamps will be working. You can walk on if you want, or we can camp out here until morning, go get gas and keep going. But I think I'd end up catching up to you about the time you pass my town anyway."

"You didn't gas up before leaving Philly?" Cassy asked, incredulous.

"I tried to, but the pumps all need power to work, so I was just hoping I'd make it home. I would have, except I had to drive slow and stop to move cars, and so on. I wish I had thought to siphon some gas before, but I'm embarrassed to say, I didn't think of it. I just hoped I'd have enough to make it home."

Cassy agreed it was better, and safer, to wait together until morning, and they settled in for the afternoon. They talked about small things like parents, schools, and work to pass the time, and James shared a box of granola bars with her in exchange for half a bottle of water. How foolish to doubt him, she thought, because he'd been friendly and now shared his food with her. Although, she noted, he hadn't really said much about himself, apparently preferring to listen to Cassy talk.

Without electric lighting, at dusk she became drowsy again. As darkness came in full, they both reclined their seats and settled in for the night. Cassy dozed off into dreams of her kids watching movies and eating microwave popcorn.

Something small and solid pressed painfully into the back of her head. She opened her eyes, but in her sleep, she had curled up facing her window. All she saw was darkness outside.

"Don't move, bitch."

"God, Jim, what the hell are you doing?" she cried, flinching away from the pain and fighting the urge to put her arms over her head—he had told her not to move.

"Can't be too careful now, Cassandra, so I checked your bag while you slept. Guess what I found?"

Cassy realized it must be her own gun pressing against the back of her head, and let out a little whimper of fear. "Don't kill me," she pleaded.

"Not only did you have food—and yet you had no problem eating *my* food—but you also had a gun. You didn't tell me you had a gun. Not nice, Cas."

"But Jim, I traded water for the food, I didn't take it," she exclaimed. "The gun is just something I carry, I didn't even think about it. Please, I swear..."

James pressed the barrel against her head even harder and cut her off. "Shut the hell up. Yeah, I traded because I didn't think you had your own food. Now I know why you didn't say anything about the gun. You were going to kill me in my sleep and take my car, weren't you?"

Cassy realized he wasn't asking her a question. It was a statement. Her mind went numb with fear. "No, Jim, I wouldn't do that, I swear."

"Here's the thing. This is a brave new world, now. I would have called 911 like always, but no power and no phones, and no cars for cops to get here in. So I think I have to handle this myself. Get out of the fuckin' car."

She reached slowly, very slowly, for the handle with trembling hands, and opened the door. James pushed the barrel into her head even harder, forcing her out of the car and into the night.

"Don't kill me, I have kids," she pleaded as she exited the car.

He got out too and kept the gun pointed at her. "So does everyone else. Most will be dead in a few days or weeks, I imagine."

James moved around the car to where Cassy stood, and grabbed her by the hair. He wrenched it hard, forcing her to move to the front of the car, and threw her face-forward over the hood. "Hands on the hood of the car, spread 'em," he commanded.

Cassy, still in mental shock at the situation, did just what he said. "What are you going to do," she cried out, fear in her voice. "Don't kill me, please!"

"I can't call the cops to deal with you. So, I'm going to deal with this myself. You basically stole my food, and you were going to steal my car, leaving me out here alone. For that, I'm going to take everything you have; your food, your bag, your water, your gun."

Cassy froze in place and her throat closed up. She tried to argue, to beg, but she couldn't make the words come out. Eyes wide with fear, she looked back over her shoulder at the man and saw him standing behind her with the gun inches from her face. He smashed the barrel across her face, cutting her cheek and lip with the front sight of the gun. Cassy cried out in pain and crumpled onto the hood. The coppery taste of blood filled her mouth. Oh god, she thought, don't let me die like this...

James snarled, "Don't look at me again, or I'll put your brains all over my windshield. As for your plan to kill me, well, I can't put you in jail. And I don't *want* to kill you—the world ain't that bad, not yet. But... Well, I can't just let you go without punishment you'll remember the next time you wanna rob someone. Can I?"

Cassy didn't reply. She couldn't think of anything to say. Instead, she cried in terror.

"Cry all you want, Cassandra; it won't help you escape justice. No, you do have to be punished. Something that'll put the fear of God into you. Punishment equal to the crime. You were going to kill me, after all. You wanted to take my life."

Cassy started to protest again, but he smacked her in the

back of her head with the pistol, dazing her. There was a moment of silence. Then Cassy felt his hand on her back. The hand moved smoothly and lightly up to her neck, then down her spine to the top of her pants. There was a *crack* and she felt a stinging pain on her buttocks. For a moment, she was confused, but then it dawned on her that he had spanked her. Amidst the inky blackness of fear, a tiny light of anger began to burn in her mind.

Crack. Crack. Crack.

"Well now," said James, and Cassy heard something new in his voice, something she'd heard before from other men, a husky edge to his tone. She knew where this was going now, and the flicker of anger grew larger.

"I do believe I know how to punish the criminal for her crime, now," James said, and it didn't escape Cassy's notice that he referred to her in the third person. "The criminal wanted to take a life. Justice demands that I take something from the criminal, something just as irreplaceable: her dignity. She should remember this lesson in the future."

James squeezed her right hip roughly, and then pressed the barrel into her head again, pinning it to the hood of the car. "The criminal should take the punishment without struggling, and without crying out," he said. "Justice must be done, here."

Cassy felt his hand slide around her waist and then down, between her legs. He grabbed her painfully down there and then moved his hand up towards the button of her pants. He didn't fumble with it, but rather, grabbed the corner of the flap and ripped hard, popping off the button and tearing the zipper apart. She cried out in pain as the canvas waistline dug into her skin. She would have a terrible bruise from that, some part of her mind decided. And again, the anger grew, but she was still helpless.

James moved the barrel to her back and yanked her

pants down around her knees. "Oh my," he said. *Crack*. Pain. *Crack*. More pain. He continued slamming his palm across her buttocks until she began to cry out.

"The criminal will now suffer her punishment," James said, voice rough and raw with excitement, and she felt his hand grip her underwear.

Nononono... How dare the bastard do this to another human being, she thought. Her anger flared into a fiery rage, driving away the darkness of the fear that had overwhelmed her. And she made a decision.

Cassy then waited until she felt James pulling her underwear down. He would be distracted then, she knew. As they slid down her legs, she slowly moved one hand over towards her body. She reached between her breasts and felt a mix of rage and joy when she found the knife there. It was just a folding pocket knife, but it only needed one hand to open.

Cassy heard the rustle of James' pants as he struggled one-handed to get his own belt undone. She felt the pressure of the gun against her back lift, then it was gone entirely, and she heard the jingle of his belt buckle. He was, for a second, using both hands to get his pants down.

And Cassy knew it was her time to strike. With a faint snap, she opened the knife and turned the blade around into a hammer grip, blade pointing down away from her thumb. She twisted as hard as she could and brought the point of the blade whipping towards her attacker. The rage within her turned into a song of savage joy as she watched the point of the blade strike him, gliding deep into his bicep.

James screamed in pain and stepped back, but his loose jeans tripped him up and he staggered. He dropped the gun as his arms flailed for balance.

Cassy bared her teeth and snarled at James as she swung the knife at him again. She aimed for his crotch, but struck his inner thigh instead, and she relished the feel of warm blood gushing over her hand.

James cried out again and fell to the ground whimpering. "Ohfuckohfuck," he said over and over, staring at disbelief as the blood spurted from his wound.

Cassy pulled her pants back up frantically and, with huge relief, found the button still attached. She buttoned back up and only then, after a deep breath, did she look down at James bleeding on the pavement. She picked up her gun and tucked it into her waistband.

"Motherfucker," she screamed, and stared at him; he looked back at her with terror in his eyes. Then her features relaxed and she smiled prettily. "Well, James, it seems your ruling has been overturned on appeal due to lack of any fucking evidence. You're just a piece of shit, James. You think because the lights are out, you can take what you want? Maybe the world will go that way now, I don't know. But right here, right now, you're going to die. You're going to bleed to death, James. Even if you somehow manage to stop the bleeding, we're still ten miles from anything. Think you can crawl ten miles with a tourniquet on your leg? Good luck."

Remembering that the car was out of gas, she walked to the car, got the keys, and angrily threw them over the railing and into the woods by the side of the road. Rummaging through his car, she found another box of granola bars and stuffed it into her bag and into the cargo pockets of her pants. He had nothing else of value in the car. Cassy put her bag on and walked back to where James lay, frantically trying to get his belt off for a tourniquet.

"James, you piece of shit. If you somehow survive, remember that this is a brave new world. Very soon, either the lights come back on or the survivors get tough. There won't be any more soft targets to plunder or rape. Remember that. And if you die, well, c'est la vie. Too fucking bad for you."

She slung the bag over her shoulder and walked on down the road, leaving James screaming for help behind her. She made sure he did not see her tears as she left.

* * *

As Cassy walked, the shock began to wear off and soon she caught her breath. She found herself shaking from the adrenaline letdown, and her spine and head ached from its sudden absence. She considered what just happened with no less horror than when it had occurred, but without the clouding of the mind that came with extreme fear. It took a while to process the event and her feelings about it.

After a half hour or so, she got off the freeway and found a hidden place to rest in the brushes of the off-ramp circle. She fixed up her pants as best she could, then tried to nap. Her mind wouldn't stop racing, and she finally gave up and pulled out her pocket journal. She flipped past the pages of now-dead day planning, none of which mattered now, and found a blank page. Writing often helped her clear her mind when she couldn't relax, letting her thoughts slow so that rest could come.

Aug. 5th: I fear the world ended yesterday and we just don't know it yet. But my mind is on something else. A man came who seemed nice, wanted to help, and I trusted him. But he was terrible, maybe crazy. I don't know. Woke me up and held me at gunpoint with my own gun, said I wanted to rob him and kill him. WTF? Said he was going to take my gethome bag because I was going to rob him, and then it got crazier still. He spanked me. SPANKED ME! Like a kid. And it gave him ideas. I think he rationalized wanting to rape me, cuz he said it would be punishment for trying to kill him. (In my sleep? How?) And he almost did it. Almost.

But right before, I got mad. Not scared, mad. Now I'm scared of the madness. It wasn't me, couldn't have been me... I wanted him dead *and gone. Got pocket knife out of bra, and waited calmly for him to slip up. He needed both hands to take off pants and then I swung for his heart, hit his arm. He backed up and I tried to cut off his raping little dick. God, still so angry... I missed tho and got his leg, hit artery. Blood all over me, felt good. Felt like power, when I was powerless.*

But I'm such a coward. I wanted to kill him so bad, but couldn't do it. Maybe I'm just soft. I should have done it. But now I'm disgusted w/ self—how could I want to murder *a man? And how could I enjoy it?! Am I a monster?*

Well part of me wants to not trust anyone anymore. He seemed nice but wasn't. What about next time? But I know plenty of nice people are out there. What would it be to go thru life not trusting anyone? No, I think I'd rather die now than go thru life like that. Maybe I can just be more careful in the future. Esp when I get my kids back! No chances w/ their safety, right? Gotta keep 1 eye open from now on, that's all. The world isn't as bad as it feels right now. Can't be, can it?

More later. Have to sleep, have to keep going. Kids and mom waiting for me to come save them. I wish hubby were still alive, he would know what to do. I can just do the best I can, I guess, and try not to lose my humanity. Someone has to keep civilization civil...

Having written down her thoughts, her mind finally quit racing and Cassy slid into a fitful, exhausted sleep.

- **6** -

0545 HOURS - ZERO DAY +1

JENNIFER ROUGE WOKE up just before dawn. She looked around her mangled apartment in a nice, rehabbed building in what used to be called Hell's Kitchen, New York. It was now full of people like her: upwardly mobile, young, and with more money than common sense. And, she knew, that was true because her expensive apartment was full of empty bottles, half-naked men and women, and sushi boxes. When the power went out, she and her friends had thrown a huge party and it got out of hand, but, of course, no police had come to shut the party down. No cars to get there and bigger fish to fry, she guessed.

She wrinkled her nose at the spill on her couch—a white leather couch that cost more than some people made in two months, but that wasn't out of her price range. She'd have to pay someone to clean that mess off.

Then she realized that she was half-naked too, except for a pair of black boyshorts. She found a shirt—not her own—and threw it on while flipping off Chad, who was groggily staring at her chest (as usual). She stepped onto the balcony to smoke. Jennifer felt relaxed, warm and fuzzy, after the night she'd had with Mark, her "best friends with benefits." Like many of her other friends who'd partied at her crib, she and Mark were on a roll last night, she remembered with a smile. Definitely a superior effort. Maybe he'd even ask her out after a performance like that...

As she lit her cigarette, she heard the sounds of cars and trucks far below, and planes in the air, and smiled. "Finally, those dipshits got the lights back on," she muttered, and gazed out at the beautiful view of the Hudson River and the distant Upper West Side of Manhattan—a morning ritual—but then her jaw dropped and she froze, disbelieving.

The city was on fire. Far across the cityscape, she saw more buildings ablaze than she could count, and the air over the Upper West Side was black. In the river were strange ships, ships with guns, and those guns were going off—and with each shot, more of the city burst into flames. She heard the roar of a jet engine and looked up, but couldn't grasp what she saw. Three small jets that looked nothing like what she saw on the news during the Gulf War raced overhead and then launched missiles into Central Park, which was ablaze.

"What the fuck," she said over and over, unable to understand what was happening.

She heard what sounded like strings of firecrackers going off below, and she looked over the railing. Down on the street were tiny people in green on one side of the street, and tiny people in gray on the other, and they were shooting at each other. A huge truck came around a street corner and let out a puff of smoke. An explosion that shook her building, even from across the street, engulfed the tiny men in green, ending the firefight. Yet, she heard more gunshots from all around.

Then she knew she had to wake everyone. They had to get out of the building while they still could, before what happened to the Upper West Side reached them. It was already coming towards them, and it might already be too late. She had to hurry. But as she turned to run inside, the whole building convulsed and swayed, knocking Jennifer off her feet. She landed on her back on the patio, looking up, and saw a huge orange and red blossom of fire burst from the building high above her.

To Jennifer, it appeared that a sort of crystal rain began to fall from the blossom of fire. Part of her thought in a detached sort of way that the rain was utterly beautiful, seeming to drift down towards her like snow in winter. One of the snowflakes landed on her, but instead of icy cold, it was burning hot and she felt it slide, sizzling, through her cheek and out the back of her neck. Glass, she realized, and watched in sudden horror as the rest of the crystal rain floated down over her.

Bloody and hurt, Jennifer screamed in pain and terror and struggled to get to her feet. On her knees, hands on the railing to help lift herself up, she saw a terrible, menacing helicopter rise into view from below. In the cockpit, the pilot smiled and then the twin chainguns on either side of the helicopter spun into life, a moment before they spit fire at her.

Jennifer's last thought in this world was, "This can't happen here, can it?"

The thought was cut off as a seemingly solid stream of bullets reached her, and her apartment; all that remained of her party was fire and a pink mist.

- 7 -

0600 HOURS - ZERO DAY +1

THE SHORTWAVE RADIO crackled again: "So, Dark Ryder, where are you? Not many folks are talking back right now. I'm bored. Talk to me."

In the LED-lit EMP-hardened underground bunker, surrounded by crates of canned and dried food and gear, a huge map of the USA, pierced by scattered multicolored push pins, was mounted on one wall. Desks with computers and multiple radios seemed like adjuncts to the map.

Glancing at the map, "Dark Ryder" chuckled. Short and slightly round, he ran his thick fingers through thin, receding hair, then wiped them on the green MMORPG tee shirt he wore. "Watcher One, you know I can't tell you that. What's the point of a secret lair if it isn't secret?"

"Roger that," said the voice on the other end with a laugh. "So, like I said, Big Apple is applesauce now. Have you heard anything about that from your other radioheads?"

"Aff, Watcher One. I have a backdoor on a commercial satlink, and copied some images from Up On High. City's being overrun by someone—I'm still working on who. A guy in Alaska said they were North Koreans, and a gamer grrl from Orlando says it's Iranians. No idea how North Koreans would get to New York, though. And they have what we leet gamers call "combined arms." Ships, tanks, planes, troops."

"Yeah, Ryder, I know what combined arms are. I heard that POTUS declared martial law, whatever good that will do her. What's the whispernet say about how the unwelcome visitors got here?"

"Guy I know in D.C. morsed me a message, old-school style," replied Dark Ryder as he adjusted his tee shirt. "Says they hit New York by ship, but he didn't know how they got past our fleet. But I think I know how."

"You're talking out your fat ass, Ryder! You don't know shit."

"True, but I got cross-ref from someone else that the whole mid and south Atlantic are dark like us."

"Yeah, man, I heard that too. And all the East Coast bases cleared out right before someone flipped the switch off. Small units scattering, taking old gear—like they knew it was coming. Shit, I gotta go dark, satellite due to come overhead stat, Watcher One out."

Ethan Mitchel, who thought of himself more as "Dark Ryder" than as his given name, leaned back in his chair. It squeaked annoyingly, but he had neglected to stock WD40 in the bunker. He gazed again at the wall map and his thoughts drifted. He didn't trust anyone, and this was truer of Watcher One than of others. Watcher had appeared just after everything went to hell and he didn't speak geek though he tried hard. Too hard, which was a red flag. Also, even though his signal was pretty weak, it wasn't because he was far away. Ethan's remote gizmos triangulated his signal to somewhere in Virginia, or at least that's where the short wave signal had bounced last. But the most damning evidence against Watcher was that he knew too much about what was happening. He had information Ethan didn't, and vice versa, so he was useful, but Watcher claimed to be some weekend warrior HAM operator. No way he should know so much.

Ethan had been staring blankly at the map, lost in thought, but now he sharpened his focus. Black pins over Ohio, the Pacific, and now the Atlantic—these showed where he thought EMPs had simultaneously occurred. That meant that only LA southward wasn't pulsed into the dark ages though they had no power because the grid was down. They could rebuild, though. The Marines at Camp Pendleton probably had generators. So there was still an island of USA somewhere.

Red pins over New York City, Anchorage, Vancouver B.C., and Orlando showed where rumors had suggested foreign troops had landed. How much of that was real, he didn't know, but New York was a certainty—he'd seen satellite images, and knew that units all over the eastern seaboard had scattered just prior to the EMP. Or EMPs, whichever.

Ethan also knew that the President had declared Martial Law within minutes of the EMP. The statement was well-written and well-read, suggesting it was prepared and practiced well ahead of time. How much did the Feds know ahead of time, and how far ahead? Could they have stopped it? Too many questions and no answers. Not yet—but Ethan was certain he'd figure out at least part of the puzzle, given time. And all he had was time, down here in his bunker. Time and a working computer loaded with twenty years of classic video games.

Dark Ryder smiled and double-clicked on his "games" folder while he waited for someone to transmit, out in the world.

- 8 -

CASSY AWOKE AS the first glimmers of sunlight shone on her face. She was flooded with memories of the horrible events of the day before and she had to stop and wait for the feelings to pass. She'd been nearly raped by a man she had foolishly trusted but had probably killed him by leaving the man to die. If he wasn't dead yet, the bastard was almost certainly going to die soon from blood loss, dehydration, or infection. She had shied away from finishing him off—she hadn't actually killed anyone before—but a part of herself that she was ashamed of felt happy at the thought of him lying on the road, bleeding life away and waiting to take his last breath.

Once the overwhelming feelings passed somewhat, she stretched and slowly got up, groaning at the pain of her stiff back and neck. She wasn't used to sleeping on bare earth and hoped she wouldn't have to do much more of it. She took a couple minutes to stretch out and limber up, then rummaged in her pack for one of the granola bars she'd taken from her would-be rapist. She chased that down with a gulp from her limited supply of water and packed up to move out.

As Cassy crept up the embankment to the freeway's guard rail, she looked around carefully. Although she was well outside of Philly, that was no guarantee she would be safe from other travelers. "To hell with people," she muttered as she searched for movement but saw none. Climbing over the railing, she got back onto I-76 and continued on her way.

For the first hour, all was quiet, and she saw no other people. Things changed, however, rather abruptly as she walked with a steady pace around a turn in the road and saw three people ahead, a couple with one child. He looked about the same age as her own son, Aidan, though she couldn't be sure from that distance. She was about to climb back over the railing to go around them, and hopefully avoid being seen, when she saw movement to the west of the family.

Four men vaulted suddenly over the railing, aiming rifles at the road family. She could hear the men shouting but couldn't make out the words. The man and woman dropped down to lie face-down on the road, arms out. Then the family man grabbed his child and pulled him down to the ground with him.

The four men surrounded the family, still shouting, still pointing death at them. One then slung his rifle over his shoulder and threw his head back, probably in laughter. He strutted up to the people on the ground, clearly cocky even from Cassy's distance, and stripped them of their backpacks. Seconds later, they melted back into the foliage west of the freeway.

It took several minutes for the family to stand up, and they clung together for a while before moving on, shoulders hunched and heads down forlornly. Cassy knew this simple robbery had probably spelled the family's death, but there was nothing she could do to help. Nor did she want to have to hurt them if they chose to try to take her own pack; She shook her head and, with a heavy heart, climbed over the railing and disappeared like a ghost.

It would not be the last such scene she witnessed, but she would never forget that one, her first. Nor would she ever forget the terrible hopelessness that painted the family's body language when they moved on. She resolved never to become like those men. "No matter the cost," she swore to herself aloud.

After regaining her composure, Cassy continued walking north on I-76, and all was deceptively quiet. Woods stretched off in all directions on both sides of the freeway. The monotony made it difficult for her to stay alert. A couple hours later, however, the road veered west following the Schuylkill River, and she could see buildings in the distance across the water. There were more cars on the road as well, probably commuting to Philly when the lights went out.

Cassy ducked behind a car and pulled the .38 out of her pack, along with its inside-the-waistband holster, and tucked it into her pants. "Let's hope we only meet good, friendly people, okay?" she asked the gun, then continued on her way.

She wove back and forth around the cars left in the road, struggling to stay alert for danger. It wouldn't be too bad yet, she mused, as it had only been a day and a half since the power crapped out. But she'd learned a lesson about being *too* trusting of other people's good intentions. As she thought about James and his Camaro, anger rose in her again and she fought to quash it. Sooner or later she would have to process what had happened with James, but now wasn't the time.

And then she saw, ahead of her, a group of perhaps a dozen men and women, systematically going through the dead cars. She glanced around and saw that to her left, on the south side of the freeway, there was a dense forest. "Time to hide," she muttered to her hidden gun because she had no one else to talk to. "Hide or use up most of my ammo right now. Better later than now."

With that, Cassie crouched low, made her way to the railing, slid down the embankment to the trees below and took cover. When she looked out from the tree line at the road, she was relieved to see no one had seen her, or if they had, at least they weren't following her. "Time to go, girl," she said out loud.

"Talk to yourself all the time, do you?" a voice responded, only a few feet from her. Cassy's heart surged as she spun around to see a young woman crouching near a bush, hidden from the road. The woman was stunningly beautiful, Cassy noted, and couldn't be more than nineteen or twenty, going by the girl's appearance and body language. She wore tight-fitting jeans, a low-cut black halter top with a white skull on it, green "skater" shoes, and a thin black jacket. Her blonde hair was long and wavy, falling to her mid back.

Cassy thought the girl would get herself into trouble looking like that if she wasn't careful. And then she shuddered as she suppressed a recent unpleasant memory along those same lines.

"Funny," Cassy said, smiling at the girl. "You live around here?"

The girl's eyes narrowed. Good girl! Not too trusting, Cassy noted with approval.

"No," the girl said hesitantly. "I live west of here. My car died, yeah? So, I'm walking. But I didn't like the look of some peeps on the road, so I bounced."

"Right," said Cassy with a grin. "Good choice. There's bad people out there now, believe me. Still headed west?"

"Yeah, but I'm staying off the road until I get past this town. I'm hungry, but not that hungry. Not yet."

Cassy thought about the girl stumbling across another

James out there and frowned. Aw hell, she decided suddenly, they were going the same direction for a while, at least, and Cassy had a gun to chase off any unwelcome attention the girl might attract. Plus, it would be nice to have company, even if that company was closer to her daughter's age than her own.

"Well, I'm Cassy. I have a bit of food if you are hungry, and if you want to walk with me for a while. Two are safer than one. I hope to get to my mom's house eventually, but I'm going to have to camp out here tonight. There's more food at my mom's—you'd be welcome to get a full tummy and rest up there if you want, before you go on your way. If you decide that's what you want to do."

The girl stiffened, and her eyes darted around once, warily. "Why would you do that, Cassy? You don't owe me. Not that I'm complaining. But what's in it for you?"

"I have a daughter not much younger than you. And I know some of the people out here are not nice. The kind of not nice that women have to worry about, especially pretty young women traveling alone. What's your name?"

"Jaz. That's what people call me, and it's good enough. You know, I don't have anything for you to steal if that's what you're thinking."

"No, Jaz. I have enough to get where I'm going. I don't need anything from you. I'm just trying to be nice, kid. Let's walk, and you can have a couple of my granola bars. Sound okay?"

Cassy walked with Jaz at a comfortable pace and was happy to give the younger woman a few granola bars for the company. Somehow helping this girl seemed to calm her ragged feelings about what she'd done to her would-be rapist.

Jaz turned out to be outgoing, funny, and smart, if naive, and Cassy felt things were definitely looking up. Better still,

Jaz loved to talk, which helped take her mind off the horrible encounter with James.

In an hour they were closer to King of Prussia than to Conshohocken—which, Jaz had informed Cassy, was the name of the urban area north of I-76 they had passed—and it was still only early afternoon.

"So, we have a decision to make, Jaz. We're away from the towns right now, which is good, but there's not enough light left to get past King of Prussia today. We'd have to camp out on the edge of the town, and I don't think that'd be safe." She decided not to mention James or the fact that he lived there. "Also, we need to decide whether to camp together. Like I said, you're welcome to join me for a while, but do you trust me enough to camp with? Things aren't all that bad yet, but they soon will be. Trust is going to matter. So you have two choices to make."

Jaz beamed a winning smile, and Cassy was again struck by how pretty the girl was. "Well, my feet really hurt. I know you saw me kinda limping. These damn shoes weren't really meant for all this. So yeah, I could camp here and rest my feet. Blisters are ugly."

"And the other thing?" asked Cassy, amused that the girl still cared about how her feet looked.

"Well, I have no reason to mistrust you, Cassy. You kinda took me in when you didn't have to, you know? And you gave me some granola bars, which you didn't have to do. You're, like, a good person. I just get that sense about you."

Cassy grinned, openly pleased at the compliment. "Well, I try to do the right thing. It doesn't always work out that way, but I still try. Okay, let's find a place to camp. Someplace out of view and maybe with some shelter."

The two of them searched for about half an hour before finding a clearing between some trees, just big enough for both to lie down with what little gear they had. The trees would block both wind and rain, if it came to that, and would hide them from anyone passing by unless they were almost on top of them. They spent the rest of the day quietly talking, and just after dusk weariness overtook them. They settled in to sleep.

- 9 -

1130 HOURS - ZERO DAY +1

SSGT TAGGART WIPED sweat from his eyes. Passing
through York had been rough, physically and mentally. A lot
of people had wanted to get out of the city, where stores
already had bare shelves, and the crowd had migrated to
Highway 30 just north of town. This made driving slow, as
they had to be careful to avoid hitting anyone.

Once they got just south of Pleasureville, a wealthy
neighborhood, things got uglier. A second small horde of
well-off suburbanites arrived at the freeway wanting the
protection of moving with armed soldiers. While there were
more of the less affluent people, the wealthy ones felt
entitled to better protection. Taggart grinned when he
remembered the Lieutenant ordering the unit to keep
moving, and the smug look falling off those arrogant faces.

Before they had gone another hundred feet, the Lt. gave
the order to halt and Taggart frowned. It turned out the Lt.
had been bought. Not by money, of course—that would be
useless to the soldiers, and soon, to everyone else. But the
wealthy suburbanites had brought stockpiles of drugs with
them. Painkillers, uppers, downers, anxiety meds,

antibiotics. These they traded to the Lt. for an escort out of York and away from the large mob of filthy peasants.

Taggart had questioned the Lt. away from everyone else, and was told sobering news: they'd be in the field without support for weeks, if not months, fighting something or someone unknown. They would need all those supplies. Taggart guessed, correctly, that the pharmacies were among the first stores cleared of merchandise, and a trade like this might mean life or death for the men later on. Dammit.

And worse, it took hours to get the civilians as far as the Susquehanna River. They could have made much better time without the civvies, who complained endlessly whenever anyone came within earshot. They were hungry, they were tired, little Suzie-Q had a blister, Agnes was unspeakably rude. Waah.

Because of the complaints, to Taggart's frustration, the Lt. gave the order to stop for the night and they circled up the vehicles. They would no doubt have to ward off the less fortunate rabble all night long, though so far they'd kept a safe distance from the civvies and the soldiers' guns.

At least they'd reach Lancaster by noon the next day, thought Taggart, and that was as far as the Lt. intended to go with these sniveling, over-privileged civilians. After that, they would make much better time up Highway 222 to I-76, and onward to New York, where their real mission lay.

- **10** -

0600 HOURS - ZERO DAY +2

AS THE FIRST mottled light of day broke through the canopy above her, Cassy stretched and smiled. She had slept great, feeling comfortable and safe. Though another day of walking lay ahead of her, she had Jaz for company and the time would fly by.

Cassy slowly opened her eyes and sat up, smiling. "Mornin', Jaz," she began but stopped halfway through. Jaz wasn't in sight. Perhaps she had gone to relieve the call of nature, Cassy thought, and she stood to stretch again.

"Jaz, hurry up," she called out cheerfully while she stretched. "We need to make at least ten miles today, should be easy."

But when she reached for her backpack, it wasn't where she left it. Her heart sped up and a cold feeling washed over her. "No, no, no... Please don't do this to me," she said as she frantically looked all around the area.

Ten minutes later she knew. Her pack was gone, and so was Jaz. "That damn bitch," spat Cassy, putting her hands to her hips in a rage. And there she felt the cool, comforting finish of her pistol. A smile crept over her face. "So, no food, no gear—but at least I was smart enough to take this out of my pack." And of course, she still had her backup knife—the one she'd tried to neuter her would-be rapist with. It was small but sturdy and sharp.

She had only another eight or ten miles to go to reach her mother's house in Chesterbrook and thought she could cross that distance in just a few of hours, even staying off the freeway. This was a relief because, although she was fine, she knew the remaining stocked food would be gone for most people sometime tomorrow; she frequented "prepper" forums, where three days of food in grocery stores was the conventional wisdom.

Okay, Cassy told herself, it was time to get going and stop sitting around bitching. She couldn't do anything about Jaz leaving with her pack. But if she ever saw that bitch, Jaz, she'd shoot her in the kneecap for what she'd done. It was less than Jaz deserved, but Cassy wasn't sure she could kill someone unless she absolutely had to. Kneecaps would have to do.

An hour later she'd gone only two miles over the rough, uneven terrain off the freeway. She was close enough to King of Prussia to be concerned about people now, and a mile back she'd seen through a gap in the trees a sign on the freeway, which read, "Cooper Area Vocational College 1 Mi." It must be just north of her, she guessed. But she was getting thirsty, and couldn't keep walking the difficult terrain without something to drink, soon. Tomorrow she'd need to find food to have the energy to make good time, but she hoped to be with her kids and her mother by then. Finding water was more urgent.

- 11 -

0600 HOURS - ZERO DAY +2

BEFORE DAWN, SSGT Taggart stowed his gear and got ready to move out while he sucked down a canteen full of terrible MRE coffee. Soon enough, he knew, even bad coffee would be a blessing, so he took a minute to relish it. That done, he relieved the watch NCO. During the five-minute briefing, he learned that one of the "rabble" civvies had infiltrated the camp looking for water, and an overeager soldier had used his knife on the intruder. As a result, the rest of the rabble was agitated and tense and had clustered just far enough away to avoid getting shot, but refused to disperse and go away. They wanted the soldier who had killed one of their own.

As the sun crested the horizon, both civilians and soldiers roused, and the mob outside the circle of Humvees grew louder, inching closer to the soldiers' encampment. To Taggart, they looked hungry and angry—a dangerous combination. He rushed to find the Lieutenant.

"Sir," he reported with a salute. Lt. Dunham nodded at him, and Taggart continued, "The civilians out there are massing up. They're hungry, sir. One infiltrated the camp last night, got himself eliminated. We need to get moving, or we're going to have to deal with them."

Dunham frowned. "Yes, Taggart. I know. Look, we are obligated to protect these over-privileged pricks we're babysitting, so until we hit the city, we can't just move out. They're slow as a day-one recruit. I need twenty minutes to whip them into any shape to move out, and even then it'll be slow going. We need to move at their speed, at least for a while."

Taggart fought the urge to curse, or at least frown, and kept his bearing in front of the Lt. "Yes, sir. Orders?"

"It's Martial Law, in case you hadn't heard. Gathering like that is unlawful. Disobeying orders is a punishable offense. Use of live rounds may be necessary, and if so, my order is this: shoot every fucking one of them. Make 'em afraid to follow us further." He paused, evaluating Taggart for a second, then continued, "Don't look so sour. I don't like it either, and those poor bastards out there are my people— my family is poor and from this region. Hell, I might have had Christmas eggnog with some of these camp followers. But we have a mission, and you have your orders."

Taggart was briefly surprised by the Lieutenant's words, and his tone, but he had the discipline not to show it. The times would get a lot rougher before they got better, and he told himself he had better get used to doing things to survive that would have got him executed two days before.

Taggart grabbed the mic to a vehicle PA system and climbed onto its roof, stretching the mic cable fully to do so, and glared at the rabble-folk. Why hadn't they stocked up at least a couple days of food like everyone else kept telling them? Damn people had no common sense, always eating out and never cooking in. Well, they'd be the first to starve, he knew, and the thought made him feel depressed and then angry. But the anger ebbed, replaced by sadness, and he realized the anger had been a cover for even more unpleasant feelings. It was a soldier's job to protect these people, not chase them off. But he didn't have the supplies to care for them, and he and his soldiers were headed toward what was likely to resemble a combat zone in New York City. And there was the fact of Martial Law. The rules were different now, whether he liked it or not, and he was a soldier—orders would be followed, no matter how distasteful. It was his duty.

His conflict resolved, Taggart let out a slow sigh and steeled himself for what might come next. He put the mic up to his mouth and clicked it on. "This is the U.S. Army. Martial Law has been declared by the lawful authority of the Commander in Chief. You are unlawfully gathered. You are required to obey lawful orders of the commander of this unit. You are hereby instructed to disperse. You are commanded not to approach the members of this unit or any persons or property under its protection or in its possession. Failure to comply will be deemed a threat to the operation of this military unit. Habeas Corpus has been suspended. You are advised that these instructions will be enforced by whatever means are required to gain compliance and ensure the continued operational capacity of this unit. And, folks, I don't like this either, but if you don't disperse or you attempt to follow us, I may have nightmares about using lethal force but your deaths will last longer. Please, disperse. Go home while you can. You have fifteen minutes to comply. That is all."

Taggart threw the mic down and jumped off the roof of the Hummer. He spent a couple of minutes going from sentry to sentry, giving each the same order: "When I sound the horn, their fifteen minutes are up. If they haven't dispersed, fire three rounds into the ground in front of them.

If they approach, shoot them, not the ground. That's an order."

He then checked his rifle and his ammo load, and mentally prepared himself for what might come next. He stood motionless, then, just staring at his watch, an old windup model. The minutes ticked by, and Taggart steeled himself to accomplish the mission he was given—even if he hated it.

Ten minutes. Six. Four. But he never got to zero, never sounded the horn, because at just over three minutes left all hell broke loose when his men simultaneously opened fire. Part of him noted with satisfaction that they were using single-fire, one round at a time just as he'd trained them. Adrenaline pumped through him and he vaulted on top of the Humvee again to see what was going on, weapon ready, but he wasn't prepared for what he saw despite steeling himself for it.

On the road, the rabble had locked arms four-abreast and had simply walked towards the unit. They must not have expected anyone to actually shoot at them, and the mistake was costing them lives. *Crack. Crack. Crack.* Bodies fell. In only a couple seconds at least a dozen of the thirty or so civilians had fallen, and the rest immediately turned to run, screaming, for their lives.

"Cease fire! Cease fire!" came the cry from Lt. Dunham, who had come from behind to stand next to Taggart. The shooting petered out, but not before a couple more people had fallen, those who hadn't fled quickly enough.

"Goddamn fools," the Lt. muttered through clenched teeth. Rage and sorrow briefly chased each other over his features, Taggart saw, but then the Lieutenant regained control and forced his face into a stony mask. "Sentries stand ready! Soldiers, get our civvies up and moving. We move out in five, whether they're ready or not."

Taggart's grief turned to anger as the vision of falling humans kept flashing through his mind. He stormed off to follow orders, to get the civilians ready. He was none too gentle about it.

- 12 -

0800 HOURS - ZERO DAY +2

CASSY HADN'T BEEN walking long when she heard the faint murmur of running water. There was a stream ahead, and she had a moment of pure joy as her thirsty body urged her to run headlong and drink deeply, but she forced herself to stop and think. The stream would be an open area, not in cover as she was now. Okay, so she'd have to stop at the tree line to get a good look around before emerging. Also, while she could drink her fill right away, it might not be clean water—a town was right next door, after all. And finally, she had no way of taking water with her. Not since that devious little bitch, Jaz, had taken her only supplies. Three problems, only one of which was easy to deal with.

Cassy sighed and moved cautiously toward the water. One thing at a time, she told herself. When she got to the edge of the timbered area, the sight that met her was welcome beyond belief—crystal clear water, and a lot of it, moving slowly through a creek. She had read that slow-moving water wasn't as safe to drink as water from the rapids. That led her to the second issue, but the same book that had told her fast water was safer than slow also told her how to filter it. That wouldn't be too hard. She could use her shirt and her hoodie to filter the water by tying one above the other—fill one with small foliage and the other with sandy soil, and it would be filtered, albeit poorly since she had no charcoal for a third layer. It would have to do. She'd drink it and pray she didn't get Giardia or some other parasite or disease from the water.

The third problem—figuring out how to carry some water with her—was the hardest. She would have used her canvas pants, tying the legs off into makeshift water bags, but she had not thought to wax them. She glumly chastised herself. Nor did she have the time and tools to make a wood or birch bark container for water. The only option that would let her keep moving without a long delay, she realized, was to find ready-made containers.

Cassy followed the stream south away from the town, keeping in cover and looking for any movement as she searched for anything she could use as a container. It didn't take her long to find a few plastic water bottles along the edge of the stream, among other trash that included crumpled beer cans and a faded, waterlogged "gentlemen's magazine." But before leaving cover, she sat down and simply waited, watching and listening. Going to get the bottles and the water would leave her exposed, and she didn't relish the thought of another conflict, or of meeting anyone. Her trust meter was just about pegged to zero, at least for the moment, she thought wryly.

A high-pitched squeal full of pain and fear echoed through the trees, and Cassy whipped her head towards the noise automatically. "That sounded like a little kid. Goddammit," she muttered, and quickly—and quietly—made her way toward the disturbance.

The stream she followed meandered to the left ahead of her, and the trees blocked her view of anything beyond that point. As quickly as she felt was prudent, staying in cover, she rounded the bend so she could see more of the stream. And as the view opened up ahead of her she saw the source of the noise: a small child now floated face-down in the stream. Maybe a hundred yards upstream from the child, on the other side of the water was a group of maybe a half-dozen adults, who were frantically running to and fro searching, but they didn't seem to see the kid in the water. Cassy decided they would never figure it out in time. If she didn't do something quickly, that kid was probably going to die. A strangled "No..." escaped her lips and she burst out of the treeline, sprinting for the water, caution to the wind.

As she emerged, one of the adults saw her and pointed, letting out a cry of alarm. The group of surprised adults edged forward, unconsciously putting themselves between Cassy and their encampment, which had several other kids, Cassy noted distractedly as she ran.

She reached the stream, which had slowed again after speeding up at the bend, and she saw the child still remained motionless. Without hesitating she leapt into the air, getting across as much of the wide stream as she could before hitting water. She landed feet-first, rather than dove, and that turned out to be a wise choice; her feet hit the rocky bed of the stream and the water was only just above her elbows. Had she dove in, she might have been hurt. Regaining her footing, she pushed off and swam quickly towards the child. Cassy wrapped one arm around the kid's neck and with her other hand flipped her over and side-stroked to the closest shore. She half-threw the girl onto the bank of the stream and got out of the water with adrenaline-soaked speed.

Within seconds, she began CPR. She didn't have to stop to think about what she was doing—the process was muscle-memory now, after the long hours of paramedic training she'd gone through with no intention of being a paramedic.

Her mother, Mandy, had said it was a waste of time and money if she wasn't going to be a paramedic, but Cassy only replied that it was an investment in self-confidence. It was the easiest way to explain it to her doubting mother.

For this little girl, though, Cassy thought as she quickly checked for a pulse, the training would be a neither a waste of time nor money.

The girl interrupted Cassy's thoughts when she abruptly began to cough hard enough to make her whole body spasm. Cassy rolled her onto her side with a whoop of joy. "Air in, water out, kid. Cough hard!"

The girl was maybe seven years old with long brown hair matted around her face. She might have been pretty enough, normally, but right now she was slightly blue and coughing hard enough that she'd probably pull some muscles. Cassy patted her head and spoke calmly, reassuringly, and took off her hoodie to drape it over the girl's shoulders.

That was when she looked up finally and noted the group of adults coming to a stop, having run from camp. A woman of perhaps thirty-five with brown hair and the same nose as the little girl swept the kid up in her arms, shrieking with joy and fright wrapped together. The child whimpered and buried her face into the woman's neck, sobbing.

Seeing this, Cassie smiled without thinking, her face lighting up with joy and relief. She barely heard the woman saying "thank you" over and over. She glanced at the others then and saw three men and two more women. The women were smiling, but the men looked tense, cautious. Cassy became suddenly nervous. Her experiences with strangers hadn't been wonderful, lately.

After a second, one of the men finally smiled too and stepped forward a couple paces, still staying a comfortable distance from Cassy, maybe four feet. "Thank you, miss. That's Jed's daughter there, and she's like our own child to all of us here. I don't want to think what would'a happened if you hadn't come along."

Cassy stood, hands carefully kept at her side, and then smiled again. "I'm Cassandra. I got kids, too—I didn't even really think about it, just jumped in." She shivered a little, still dripping wet.

"I'm Frank. The girl's Kaitlyn, and her mom's Amber. You look cold. We got a fire goin', and seeing as how you just saved Amber's girl I think we could spare a cup o' joe and a little food to warm you up, but that's all we got." He smiled, his eyes crinkling as well, but added, "That, and some guns, but we can't share those of course. Figure we'll be hunting our food soon enough."

Although Cassy didn't miss the implied warning when he mentioned their guns, all she felt was relieved. She was hungry and thirsty, and they seemed genuinely grateful. Then she thought about the times she'd been wrong, and resolved to keep alert. Just in case. "That'd be great, Frank. I haven't eaten since yesterday afternoon, nor had water. I was thinking about how to filter and carry some from the stream when I heard Kaitlyn shriek and went running."

They walked back to the camp, just upstream, and Cassy saw they had two army surplus bivouac tents. They were huge things made of sturdy canvas, way too heavy to carry any distance. They had cast iron pots and pans, ice chests, racks of bottled water.

"You come prepared. That's a lot of gear to haul out here without a car," Cassy said. Her curiosity showed, and Frank chuckled.

"Yeah, I suppose it would be, but we drove it out here. Well, the cars died just outside of town on our way to a weekend campout, and we thought it prudent to stay out of town. Just in case, right?"

"Smart. Frank, if the lights don't go back on tomorrow,

that town won't have one store with food on the shelves. Hell, people are already getting unruly," she added, and her face scrunched into a grimace as she suppressed a sudden flashback to her encounter with James.

"So why are you going to town? Family?" Frank asked, then sat on a log by a small fire.

"No, I'm going around it. I need to get to Chesterbrook, that's where my mom and kids are. From there, I don't know what we'll do but we'll be together," she said, unwilling to mention her huge stockpile of food and gear outside of Lancaster.

A woman emerged from one of the huge tents. Cassy saw she had a pistol in a holster on her hip and a frown on her face as she looked at Cassy warily. "You brought her to our camp? Dammit Frank, my dad told me you were an idiot."

Cassy saw Frank tense as he replied with an even voice, "Shut up, woman. She saved Kaity's life, and we're thanking her the best we can. It's just some food and water, so calm down or go the hell away."

"You best give her some of Amber's food and water then, let her pay this woman back. It better not come out of the stockpile. We need to make that last, you idiot."

Cassy didn't like where this was going, and slowly slid her hand closer to the pistol hidden at her side. Things are different now, she reminded herself. "I sure don't mean to take anything I didn't earn or wasn't given," she said to the woman. "I'm Cassy, and I'll be moving along in just a few, I promise."

The other woman's eyes narrowed at Cassy, and one side of her mouth rose in a snarl. "I'm Mary," she said with no hint of friendliness. "Thanks for saving Kaitlyn, but that's not my daughter. You don't get to take food out of my own kid's mouth. Understand me, Cassy?"

Cassy let out a deep breath that she hadn't realized she

was holding, and let her shoulders visibly slump. "I got it. I have kids too, and sure wouldn't like anyone to take their food. I'll eat what's offered, but then I'm moving on. You have my word."

Mary smiled, but it didn't reach her eyes. "Well then. Enjoy your visit. And Frank? Keep it in your pants." She turned and walked briskly back into the tent.

"Damn. Sorry about her, Cassy. We lost a child a year back, things haven't been the same between us since. But Mary's a good woman. Not that you'd know it from what you just saw."

Cassy forced a chuckle and a smile. "I'm sorry to hear about your loss. I can't imagine how I'd be if I lost my kids. I won't take what she said personally."

Frank opened his mouth and then snapped it shut. Opened it again, and snapped it shut. Cassy just sat quietly, enjoying water and a bite to eat as it was brought to her. She figured he'd either say what was on his mind or bring up something light if he decided to talk about something else.

Finally, he said, "We've had a problem or two with other people. That's another reason Amber's so protective of her girl, and why my wife is all put out about you." He then looked at Cassy and raised one eyebrow, expectantly.

Cassy nodded somberly and replied, "Oh? What sort of trouble?"

"Well, with all the cops more or less out of commission right now, we had a couple times people stumbled by and found one or two of us alone. By a couple, I mean two times. The first time, three men tried to grab Amber and Kaity, but we heard the ruckus and got to them right quick with our guns out. We didn't have to shoot 'em, though. They saw the guns and bounced out. The second time we were carryin' all this stuff in trips from the road. Jed and I came back to the car and found four guys who looked pretty thuggish going through our stuff. That time we had to fire a shot, but just a warning shot you see. They didn't run, but they did leave, yelling threats."

"Wow. And that was all just after the lights went out, huh?"

"Yes. Listen, Cassy... You seem like a right and decent person. You saved Kaitlyn, and I'm grateful. But a woman traveling alone, especially one as pretty as you... Well, you might draw the wrong type. It's going to get you into trouble you don't deserve."

Cassy watched Frank's eyes the whole time. Not once did they slide over her body the way almost all men did, consciously or not. He was a good man, she had thought in the beginning, and now she was sure of it.

Still, could she trust him and all the people in his group? Her trust hadn't been rewarded in recent days.

On the other hand, Frank's group seemed strong and capable. Their leader seemed to have a good head on his shoulders. Having a group would be damn important on the farm. She couldn't do all the work herself, especially not with two kids to watch. Maybe this group was what her mom would call "divine intervention." It certainly felt like synchronicity. A group would be stronger and safer than Cassy all by her lonesome.

And they had kids. Cassy briefly watched them playing and smiled as she thought of her own kids. Yeah, maybe she could help them and they could help her. It seemed like a win/win situation and she didn't think she could just leave good people with good kids out in the wild to die, not if they'd take her help.

"Frank, I like you. I appreciate the concern. And I think your wife lucked out—you're easy on the eyes, yourself. More importantly, you got a good bunch of people here. Even Mary, though she was pretty rude, well she's scared for her family. I don't blame her. I'm scared for my daughter, too. So... I got a proposition for you."

Frank waggled his eyebrows at her, lips turned up into a smirk.

"No, not that kind of proposition," Cassy giggled. "But seriously. I have a house not too far away. It's in pretty rural territory, far enough from the city that mobs of starving people won't be too much of an issue. And I have years of food laid up. I have a HAM radio and guns—and the radio was in a faraday cage, so whatever turned out all the lights won't have fried it."

Frank interrupted, "What's a faraday cage?"

Cassy smiled and knew in her bones that these people needed her help, and she theirs, if she could just convince them. "Well, you know how your microwave doesn't fry everything near it? That's because of a mesh that completely encloses it—you can see some of that mesh in the front glass if you look closely, right? Okay, well a faraday cage is basically the same thing, but instead of keeping energy *inside*, it blocks any energy coming in from the *outside*. Same technology, but it doesn't have to be as complex as a microwave."

"Got it. That's a ten dollar answer to a two dollar question, miss, but it sounds like you know your stuff. You weren't one of those people on that 'Apocalypse Preppers' show, were you?"

"Doomsday, not Apocalypse, and no. I just wanted to be ready for emergencies like hurricanes, riots, whatever. That stuff *does* happen, you know. Ask anyone in New Orleans a few years ago. Anyway, I'm getting off track."

Frank eyed Cassy, not exactly warily, but definitely revising his opinion of her, Cassy thought. Hopefully for the better.

"Anyway, it turns out to be a lucky thing, my getting

ready like that. I have enough food there to take your whole group in, and keep little bellies full for at least a year or two with all of you and my family. And you said it yourself, going there alone is going to get rough for a lone female of my obvious grace and beauty," she said, dramatically flipping her hair over her shoulder.

Frank chuckled. "Stop that, I reckon you aren't one of those fancy types. You have a good head on your shoulders. And I hear what you're asking. I'd have to ask the others, but I think I can tell you what most of us will say. And that's a polite 'no thank you.' We're all pretty set on cruising the woods between here and Philly, to be close when rescue comes. I figure they'll get to Philly real quick because it's so big."

Cassy's heart sank. Their choice would leave them hungry and in danger, but that was their own decision. She felt truly bad for the little kids though.

"Well, talk to them and see. But I'm heading out in half an hour or so. I can make good time now that I'm rested and hydrated. Frank, I want you to know your group is welcome at my house if you change your mind down the road..."

Cassy then told Frank in detail how to get to her homestead, without writing it down for him. It occurred to her that a map might find its way into the wrong hands. Frank thanked her, and the group spared two water bottles and stuffed her cargo pockets with food and snacks before she went. Cassy decided to eat as little of it as possible, instead foraging for the rampant wild food growing everywhere. Leafy purslane, easy-open Hickory nuts, and black elderberries were all in season, and grew everywhere.

Cassy felt bad about taking their offered food—they would need it themselves soon enough. But she would need it too, and the world would be a very different place tomorrow when the stores were fully barren and the hungry times began. In the end, she cared more about reaching her children than she did about this group. The thought left her feeling dirty, and she quickly stuffed those feelings in a box deep inside herself, right next to the box for her friend Tyrel, and for James, whom she had probably killed. Time enough for guilt and sorrow when her family was safe, damn it.

- **13** -

MANDY STOOD IN front of her open cupboards, just staring. She wore a blank expression, but her thoughts churned. The cupboards were nearly bare. The frozen food was gone, and the stuff in the fridge was long gone or already bad. Dinner tonight would be PB&J sandwiches with instant Tang for drinks. Tomorrow the last of the eggs and muffins would be all that was left, and after that...

She shook her head, clearing her mind of the thoughts. Do something else, she told herself. Maybe a neighbor could spare some food. Yeah, right. "Okay, kids, stay inside while Grandma goes outside to look around, okay?"

The kids were playing Go Fish, and their only reply was a grunt of acknowledgment, in unison. That made Mandy smile. The kids were so alike in some ways, yet so different in others.

Mandy unlocked the door and stepped outside onto her front porch, and looked around. The neighborhood was silent. Middle-of-the-woods silent. She saw no one anywhere, and for a moment thought perhaps she and the kids were the last people on earth. What a sad idea, she mused, then walked towards a neighbor's house. Not the guy who threw the tire iron—she was afraid of him—but to the other side was an elderly couple who had always been friendly with Mandy, and always had treats for Mandy's grandkids. Nice people.

She knocked on the door politely. No answer. She waited a moment and then knocked harder. From behind the door, she heard a noise, loud and metallic. She'd seen enough movies to recognize a shotgun being racked.

"Get away, Amanda," came the gravelly old voice of Mr. Pease. She heard Mrs. Pease, too, sternly telling her husband not to shoot that nice lady. He snarled at his wife, "I won't unless she tries to come in. Dammit, woman, get out of the way."

Mandy steeled herself and said in a loud, clear voice that was as relaxed and friendly as she could manage, "Mr. Pease, I'm not coming in, I promise. I'm too old for all that nonsense, you miserable goat!"

From behind the door, she heard the man laugh. He and Mandy had always shared a sort of gruff humor, and Mrs. Pease was forever telling her husband to be nicer, not understanding the banter for what it was.

"Okay, then I guess I won't shoot you," he retorted. More seriously, he asked, "What do you want, Amanda?"

"I have my grandkids, you know, and they're awful hungry and getting hungrier. I was wondering if you had some soup or bread. Anything you could spare, really. Cassy should be here soon, but until then we're short on edibles. I only have those brownies you made me last week. I don't think they'll ever go bad, but then again, they don't qualify as food!"

Mr. Pease replied with no humor in his voice, only regret. "I'm sorry, Mandy. We don't have enough for ourselves. I've nothing to give you. I would if I could, you know that right?"

Mandy heard the regret in the old man's voice and sighed. "Alright, old man. I understand, truly. Please don't feel bad. I'm sure we'll figure something out. You and Mrs. Pease just hang in there, okay? If you need help with anything, let me know. Anything but food, that is. Right?"

Those poor nice neighbors would be dead soon if the lights didn't come back on, she knew. She walked away feeling sorrow for them—and more afraid for her own family than she had been before. Hungry times were coming for everyone...

- **14** -

MANDY LOOKED AROUND her living room. Brianna lay on the couch, half awake, while Aidan was barely asleep on the loveseat. Mandy sat in the recliner, a blanket over her lap. The .38 revolver was on her lap too, under the blanket. The kids were exhausted from having too little food to keep up their usual frantic pace, but they were having difficulty sleeping nonetheless.

That was because, about an hour ago, they'd heard the first scream, followed by a loud bang. Seemingly at random after that, they heard more screams here and there from nearby houses. That was the reason she'd put the kids in the living room with her—so she could keep an eye on them. Mandy was afraid but tried not to show it to the kids. People were hungry and thirsty out there, and already they had started in on one another, taking matters into their own hands.

Brianna, who had been lying half awake, sat bolt upright, eyes wide with fear. "Grandma, I heard something outside," she whispered, voice raw with fear.

It made Mandy sad to hear that fear in her voice, but it

made her afraid, too. Was someone outside, looking for a way in? Her mind raced, thinking on whether she'd locked all the doors and windows, despite having checked them twenty times or more that night. "Wake your brother," she whispered back, "and if anything should happen you take him and run out the back to the toolshed, understand?" She tried to keep the fear from her voice, and failed.

Bang, bang, bang. Someone pounded hard on the front door. As Brianna squealed in panic, Mandy's hand slid to the revolver on her lap, and suddenly the only thing she could hear was the pounding of her heart in her ears. She froze, unsure what to do. She had no experience or training for this sort of thing. She noted in confusion that she couldn't see well, like her vision had narrowed to almost pin-point focus. She didn't see Brianna dragging Aidan out of bed. She only saw the front door. Everything else was blacked out.

There was a terrible *boom*, and the door handle seemed to disintegrate. The front door creaked slowly open as Mandy drew the pistol from under the blanket.

- 15 -

2200 HOURS - ZERO DAY +2

BITS OF DOOR handle skittered across the floor and came to rest, as the door creaked open, followed by a terrible silence. Grandma Mandy held the small .38 revolver in both hands and aimed it at the door, but her hands shook as her brain reeled and tried to catch up. She had no experience dealing with the kind of raw terror that now pumped adrenaline through her.

As the door swung open, Mandy saw a tall man in the doorway, but she couldn't register any details about him— her mind focused solely on the sledgehammer in his hands. As he stepped through the doorway, Aidan and Brianna screaming and running barely registered in her mind.

The man stopped moving, however, transfixed by the pistol pointed at his chest. Finally, he broke the silence, saying, "Why don't you put that down, lady? I only wanted some food, and I thought this house was empty like the others." He shifted his grip on the maul in his hands, but otherwise looked calm. His voice was steady as he spoke.

Mandy struggled to make sense of his words. They sounded like English, but it took a few seconds to penetrate as her mind re-engaged itself. Her food, he wanted her food, the kids' food. "Go away," she said sternly as the fear began to slip away, replaced by anger. "We don't have any food, either, and as you can see the house isn't empty. This is *my* house and *you* aren't welcome here."

"Listen, lady, I'm not here to hurt you. It's just that most of the people around you are gone, and I'm trying to find something to feed my kids. Blake and John, they're three and five, and they're hungry. You got kids, you know. Can't you share just a little bit? I need something for them, not for me. I'll go without. Please..."

Mandy hesitated. She wanted to help the guy, and it would be the Christian thing to do, but who knew how long it would take Cassy to get here? Who knew when there would be more food?

Her thoughts were interrupted when Aidan's voice sounded behind her. "Grandma, can't we help him just a little?" His voice cracked as he said it and he struggled not to cry.

"I want to help you, mister, but I have two kids here who are hungry. I'm sorry, and I'll pray for you. We'll all pray for you and your family. But that's the only help I can give you." Although she still held the pistol, she allowed the barrel to drop. She didn't want to shoot anyone, after all. Please God, she prayed, let this man leave in peace.

The man frowned. He looked down at his feet, body tense, but then relaxed his shoulders and looked up at Mandy. "God bless you for the prayers, ma'am. I'll take what I can get. But be careful, you got kids to think about and some of the folks going house to house don't much mind if there's people in them. They aren't all taking "no" for an answer. Okay? The next guy at your door might not be the God-fearing sort." The man slung the giant hammer over his shoulder, turned, and left.

Mandy sat with a knot of fear in her stomach as the man's words bounced around in her head. "New plan, kids. Grab blankets and all the food we have left, and get into the back bedroom. Aidan, find me a hammer and some nails in the kitchen, would you dearie?"

- **16** -

0600 HOURS - ZERO DAY +3

CASSY STRETCHED AS the sun came up. She had slept better than the previous night, as following the stream kept her in woodlands that offered a lot of materials to set up a small fire and a lean-to shelter. It had taken a little longer to set up than it had during practice because the only tool she had was her folding knife, which made it laborious to strip bark and heartwood for cordage and tinder. She was pleased with the results anyway. Damn, paying attention in that class had been a real good idea, she mused.

The downside to following the only source of fresh water was that she'd gotten lost. She knew in a general way what direction she had to go, but here there were no street signs, no clear view of what lay ahead. The ground undulated, trees blocked everything beyond a few feet, the stream meandered. In nature there are no straight lines, she laughed, remembering the words of her woodcraft instructor.

Cassy refilled her plastic water bottles in the stream and laid them on the rocks in the sunlight. She'd heard this would at least kill any bacteria in the water, which looked clear enough. She knew, though, that any body of water could have some nasty little bugs in it, even if it looked sweet and pure.

While the water slowly heated in the bottles, she went around the perimeter of her camp, some twenty yards out, and checked the simple deadfalls and snares she'd set up with twigs, rocks, and rough bark cordage. Most were still untouched, so she triggered them and moved on to the next. One snare was gone. She again cursed Jaz for taking her backpack with all the fine paracord in it; the bark "twine" just hadn't been strong enough for whatever critter got snagged. But the last trap, a simple figure-4 deadfall, held a surprise. A rabbit lay under the deadwood weight, crushed to death. Cassy whooped with joy and her growling stomach leaped with anticipation as she thought of sizzling rabbit for breakfast. She'd hold the camp's food gifts from yesterday for later.

She brought the rabbit back to her camp and stoked the fire. She dressed the rabbit, hanging it by its hind legs and making quick, practiced work of it. At home, she kept hides for tanning, but she had neither the time nor the tools, right now. Finally, she set up a simple spit over the fire and put the rabbit over the happy fire.

While that was cooking, Cassy searched the area in the bright light of day and found some wood that, with only a little work, would make a passable rabbit stick. About eighteen inches long and slightly curved, it was balanced enough to throw accurately, she found. With any luck, the rabbit stick would let her catch a small critter or two unawares while she traveled—she had no intention of firing her revolver unless she absolutely had to, because of the noise and her limited supply of bullets.

Cassy returned to the roasting rabbit, which she'd been turning every so often, and thought it done enough to eat her fill; what remained, she would leave behind for the scavengers. She sliced off thin bits of rabbit and made sure each sliver was cooked since wild rabbits often had parasites. When she had enough slivers to fill her, she ate it quickly and chased it down with water and a couple of the berries and leaves she'd foraged along the way.

She put out the fire, tore down her lean-to, and retrieved her water bottles. She found what had to be more or less west by the sun, and headed out with renewed energy and raised spirits.

Cassy spared a thought for what a morale raiser a simple hot meal could make, and filed that away for future reference.

* * *

Cassy followed the stream for what had to be miles. She knew her pace count, the number of steps it took her to go one hundred yards across mostly even ground, but the terrain was far from mostly even. She guessed she had gone about four miles, but knew that was misleading because she'd kept the stream in sight as she walked and it wandered back and forth. She, therefore, didn't know exactly where she was, but the stream went mostly westward and would eventually lead to a bridge, and a road. It was also the only source of water with which to refill her bottles.

The stream swerved abruptly south, which was not at all in the right direction, and she had a choice to make. "Damn," she said aloud, "do I cut west or keep following this, hoping it changes direction again?"

In the end, she decided it must just be going around higher ground, and kept following the stream. If it didn't turn after a mile or two, she could backtrack, but wanted fresh water available more than she wanted to save an hour of time.

Shortly before noon, her gamble paid off when the stream swept back towards the northwest, in the direction she needed to go. With a thanks to the powers that be, Cassy cut across to her right, heading northwest, intent on shaving some distance off the travel and meeting back up with the stream a short time later. After nearly half an hour, she reached the edge of the woods along the stream and smiled at the thought that her direction sense was improving.

And then she saw that near the stream was a mom-and-pop gas station, and that meant a road. Her little smile edged into a huge grin, and she squatted down to wait, watch and listen. "If this luck keeps up," she muttered, "then I'll find Jaz in there with my pack, a beer, and a bag of chocolate. Please, God, let there be chocolate."

Then she realized she was talking out loud, and clamped her mouth shut as she waited. And waited. But after half an hour she still saw no one and heard nothing, so she crept along the edge of cover to a position behind the store. She was about to move out in a crouching rush when she saw a camera covering the rear of the store. By reflex, she froze—anyone inside would see her on the camera. But then she nearly laughed out loud when she remembered there was no power. And just as quickly, felt sad that all she remembered that went along with the grid had come down. Just get on with it, she told herself and moved out, putting other thoughts behind her.

Cassy reached the back of the store and saw that the rear door was closed. No lock on it, but no handle either so it must only be opened from inside. She crept along the wall of the building, around the side, and crouched when she came to the corner leading to the front of the store. She peered around and saw the station had only two pumps, neither of which was lit up of course. But rather than the huge plate glass windows of a modern gas station, there were only two moderate-sized windows on the front and a single glass entry door. She crawled to the first window and, exposing as little of herself as possible, looked inside.

The interior was completely ransacked. Probably everything she could eat or drink was long gone, but she decided it was worth the time to check it out anyway, just in case. She went to the second window and repeated the process, but still saw no movement inside. Only then did she feel confident going through the door, which was slightly ajar. As she looked at it, heart beating faster, she cursed herself for not taking some tactical combat classes. She was aware that doorways were terribly dangerous places to be, but didn't know the "best" way to handle it. So, taking three deep breaths, she rushed through the door, inside, and darted to the left away from the door and counter. She then crouched and paused to listen.

She didn't have to wait long. "Well hey there, lady," came a voice from the counter, and she spun in place, wishing she had come in with her gun drawn.

Sitting behind the counter reading an adult magazine was a man who looked her over without bothering to take his hiking-boot-clad feet off the counter. He was pretty average in height and build from what Cassy could see, and wore jeans, a t-shirt, and a sheepskin jacket. Dark hair, dark eyes, average looking. She didn't see any tattoos, which made her feel a little better. Better yet, she didn't see any weapons pointed at her. That was a good sign...

"I didn't see you there, mister. Sorry for barging in."

"No problem. I'm just camping out here. Good shelter, lots to burn. But as you can see, there isn't any food in here. Hell, even the dog food is gone. So's the water, soda, and worst of all, the liquor's gone too. There's nothing here for you." The man then smiled at Cassy, baring his teeth, and she didn't think he looked friendly at all, anymore.

"Damn. Well, I'll be looking around for anything I can use, and then be off. I won't look for food, scout's honor. It's just that I got robbed, and I need a few things. All I saved was my little pocket knife." Because screw this guy, he didn't need to know she was armed.

The man took his feet off the counter and stood from the little clerk's chair he'd been lounging on. He picked up a backpack from behind the counter and set it next to the register. "Everything worth having that's left here is in my bag. That makes it mine. And seeing as how you're unarmed and all, I don't think I'll let you take any of it. Shove off, lady. Unless you want to earn loot some other way, it's time you move on—and you don't look like the kind to trade that way. My buddies will be back soon and they don't *trade* at all, if you get my drift."

A chill went up Cassy's spine as she recalled the scene in the Camaro, two or three days and one collapsed civilization ago. "Fine, I'll go. But I'm not leaving without what I need, and they're things you can spare. A map, some shoelaces, and fishing line if there's any here."

The man stared at her. Finally, one corner of his mouth turned up and his eyes lost their granite focus as he seemed to come to a decision. "Yeah, fine. Maps are by the back door there, and you can look for the rest yourself, but then you need to go. I'd be quick about looking because I really don't want you here when my friends get back."

Cassy nodded and then moved quickly up and down the aisles, starting with the one in front of the window, then the others. She grabbed up six pairs of shoelaces, two BIC lighters, and came to the fishing supplies. She grabbed two packs of small hooks and a spool of line without looking at the sizes or test weight of the line. Lastly, she grabbed a map from the rack at the back of the store near the counter.

Then her eyes fixed on the display case at the counter, which held knives of different shapes and sizes, bigger and more useful than her pocket knife. She was about to ask about them when the man's head whipped towards the bay windows.

"Damn, time's up lady. Go now, or I think you won't be leaving at all."

Cassy could hear the panicked edge to the man's voice, and sprinted towards the back door praying it would open. Thankfully it did, and just as she heard the front door opening several aisles over, she pushed it slowly open just wide enough to slip out.

"Damn, Mike, you look like you seen a ghost. What's going on?" said someone she couldn't see.

The last thing Cassy heard as she slipped out the back was the man behind the counter saying, "No one here but us chickens, Bret."

She sprinted to the tree line and didn't slow down until she was well beyond. She ducked behind a large tree and pulled out her pistol, glanced around either side of the tree to be sure she had not been followed and then slid panting to the ground to rest against her sheltering tree.

She was happy to be free but berated herself for being reckless. She should have checked more carefully before going into the gas station, damn it, and the only thing that saved her from being either captured, dead, or shooting her way out had been the fact that the man in the store was a decent guy. And, she told herself, such decent people would be getting rarer by the day now that the food was mostly gone. Even good people would do terrible things when desperate to feed their children.

Part of her wondered just how far she would go in that situation, but she didn't like the thoughts the question led to, so she stuffed it away and buried it inside a mental box for later. After all, she'd probably find out soon enough.

Still, her spirits were raised. Her recent experiences with people had not been all negative, and her self-identity held strongly to the belief that she was a good person; finding other good people gave her hope that she could stay so, even in these dire straits.

Once she caught her breath, Cassy took everything she had foraged out of their wrappings, save for the hooks, and tossed the crinkly, noisy plastic. She stuffed everything but the wrappers back into her cargo pockets and set out for the stream again.

It was slow going, but she guessed it to be a half hour later when she came to a large, four-lane bridge. Her heart soared, as now she could figure out just where the hell she was and get reoriented towards her mom's house, and her kids.

Though she wanted to walk right up to the road, she forced herself to be calm and careful. Yet again she waited to watch and listen, but this time she also circled as far as she could from within the trees. She wanted to look at the bridge and the opposite tree line from different angles. Only when she was *sure* there was no one nearby did she cautiously step out from among the trees to approach the road. She saw the name of the stream posted by the bridge, and a road sign. Then she slipped back into the cover of trees and pulled out the map.

And cursed out loud. Oh, for God's sake, when she had gotten lost she had traveled too far south. She was *still* ten miles from Chesterbrook, now south of the town at Highway 3 just before it went through Ridley Creek State Park. If she had kept going west, she would have walked right into the sleepy town of Edgemont, which was now probably anything but sleepy. It wasn't all bad, though; she could follow the stream north for quite a ways, move a little cross backcountry, and then be at an unlabeled system of streams that drained *toward* Chesterbrook. There was no way she could get lost now unless she had to move away from the water for some reason.

* * *

Jaz again cursed her luck. Nothing was going right, damn it. First she'd gotten lost after lifting that one chick's backpack, only to find there were only some granola bars and a half-eaten MRE in it, aside from crap like string and duct tape. And then she had stumbled right into the camp of three totally hickerbilly rednecks, and they didn't let her go. Oh, they fed her some great-tasting rabbit and filled her with water and booze, which was totes amaze, but then they did what lots of guys did to her. She didn't mind that, so much— it was more or less what she expected from guys. No, the worst part was that they hadn't showered in *who knows how long*, and they were all hairy. It was one thing to give it up for the quarterback or frat guys because they always gave her a ride home and invited her to the next great party. These retro rednecks, though, were an entirely different story.

Still, they had guns and promised to keep her safe. They said people were starting to shoot first, just to get stuff like her granola bars. She sure didn't want that to happen. And anyway, they were pretty nice to her, other than smelling bad. At least they were gentle with her when they did what guys do. And they fed her and looked like they could stay fed out here in the woods even if the lights *never* came back on. Yeah, she could always just close her eyes... Besides, when something better came along, she would trade up. Always trade up, her mom had told her. To Jaz, this was just another chance to start over.

But now they were using her for other, more dangerous

tasks. For example, going into the camp they'd just found, which had three families and a bunch of ice chests. The people didn't look hungry, and they had awesome tents. Tents her guardians wanted, whatever it took.

So, they had loaded her up with a plastic pouch full of rabbit meat and told her to get everyone in that camp together around the fire. Talk to them, they said. Use your charms, they said. This was so stupid, and yet there she was about to stroll into camp with a smile and a bag of rabbit. Like, what if they just shot her? She'd just have to scrunch up her courage and do it.

She got to where she could just see the camp, and crept forward to watch. Just like the rednecks said, there were three couples and three kids in two huge Army-style tents. And there was food, or at least a lot of coolers. Briefly, she watched the kids playing with a Frisbee like they were on vacation or something. The adults laughed and cheered. They seemed nice, but there was no way she was going to risk getting kicked out of *her* group for these peeps. So she stood, messed with her hair a bit to get it looking nicer and get the twigs out, and then straightened her top and jeans to look *just so*. The women might hate her, she thought with a smile, but the men would do anything she asked if they thought they could get her pants down, even if they wouldn't do so with their wives there, and all. Men were the easiest to deal with. So, she waited until all three women were on the other side of the tents and then briskly walked out towards the men.

* * *

Frank sat with Jed and Mike around the fire, cheering the kids as they played Frisbee. He was in a good mood because they had caught some fish, and one of the traps bagged them an actual, honest-to-god turkey. There'd be good eating tonight.

He was roused from his thoughts when Jed nudged him with his elbow, and Frank saw that Jed was looking beyond the kids. Frank looked over and saw what had Jed's attention, a young woman coming out of the trees.

"What do you suppose a girl like *that* is doing out here, Frank?" said Jed, grinning.

"Damn good question, Jed. Why don't you ask your wife to go find out?"

Jed frowned and glared at Frank out of the corner of his eye. "Don't be like that, Frank. There's no harm in looking, and she's a looker for sure. But maybe she needs help. We should find out, right? The Christian thing to do, and all that."

Frank rolled his eyes. Jed might be lecherous, but he wasn't a cheater so far as Frank knew. He was right about the woman, though; she was stunning. As the thought hit him, his eyes darted over to where their wives were prepping the turkey on the other side of camp. He figured as soon as they saw what was going on they'd be over in a flash. The thought made him smile.

Jed stood up first, greeting the girl with a wave. Michael was only a second behind Jed. So, with a sigh, Frank stood as well and waved while the girl came within easy speaking distance.

"We're not buying any," Frank said, forcing a smile.

Jed chuckled. "Don't be like that, Frank. Everything okay, miss?"

The girl glanced between each of the three men, and Frank realized she was sizing them up. Then she smiled at Jed, and it lit up her face. She was even more beautiful smiling, and Jed clearly ate it up because he stuck out his hand.

"Hi, I'm Jaz," said the girl as she looked right into Jed's eyes. "No, no help. I got me a rabbit, but after I saw you had kids, I thought I'd see if you needed the leftovers. Great looking kids you got. They definitely take after their dads." She smiled again.

Behind Frank, Michael muttered, "Every damn time, Jed," before stepping forward to introduce himself. "I'm Michael, and Don Juan here is Jed. The surly, quiet guy is Frank. I'm glad you're okay."

Jaz looked over to where the women were and nodded. "Pleased to meet you. I wouldn't have come over, but then I saw you had some other girls here. I don't walk up to strange men in the woods!" She laughed and looked over to Jed out of the corner of her eye, still smiling. "It wouldn't be safe otherwise, right?"

A voice careened through the camp. "What do we have here?" Amber asked as she walked quickly toward the group.

Damn and damn, thought Frank. He bolted to his feet and intercepted Amber, blocking her path. He leaned over and whispered, "You better not draw that damn pistol again, Amber. Ain't no call for that. You pull it again, you better use it, and it better be justified." Then Frank turned to smile at Jaz and returned to his seat.

Jed took a step away from Jaz and turned to his wife. "Well, hon, Jaz here just came out of the woods and offered up some rabbit for the kids. Says she has more than she can eat. Isn't that nice of her?"

Amber smiled as she looked at Jaz, but Frank thought her eyes looked wary. "Hi, Jaz. I'm Amber, Jed's wife." She motioned the other two women, who were a few steps behind her. "This is Mary and Tiffany, who are married to these other two louts. So what brings you to our lovely camp, and when will you be moving along?"

Jaz looked down, then back at Amber. "I'm just moving

through, going to Philly to get to my dad's. There's no food out there, but lots of bunnies and so on out here, so. Anyway, I just thought maybe your kids might like some fresh meat? Maybe trade for some fish, or a water bottle. And I thought you could tell me what you've heard. Everyone wants to know, and no one has answers. Then I'll move right along."

Amber smiled, and Frank thought again what a great woman Amber was, despite having grown territorial of Jed in the last few years. No business of his, he reminded himself. He and Jed might be friends, but damn if he could figure out why she was with Jed. But of course, theirs had been a shotgun wedding, which explained a lot.

"Oh, well, come on and sit down, dearie! Of course you can swap with us. I'm sure you're tired of rabbit by now, and we got a mess of fresh fish and turkey. You just come sit by me and Mary over there, okay?" She turned to Tiffany and continued, "Be a dear and get the pan, and a couple of fish, would you, please? I'll wash your dishes tonight."

Tiffany smiled, her round cheeks flushing, and she went off toward the supplies. The other adults moved their rifles out of the way and leaned them against the nearest tent, then sat around the fire, and everyone began talking at once. Jaz worked to win over the women while the wives surrounded her so the men couldn't be near her. Frank watched the display with a wry smile.

Of course, no one knew anything solid about what caused the grid to collapse, and the conversation fell to speculation. This went on all through the light meal of fish and rabbit. Sometime during the conversation, Michael's five-year-old son, Nick, crawled into Jaz's lap and began to doze. Abruptly, Jaz's smile was gone and she snapped her mouth closed so hard they could hear it.

"What's wrong, sweetie?" asked Amber warily.

Jaz looked about ready to cry. "Nothing... It's just that

you guys have *such* nice kids, and you know, you're all being so nice to me. I'm not used to that. I grew up on my own, and y'know, peeps just aren't that nice to each other where I'm from."

Frank's scalp tickled, and his mind raced. What did she just say? Then it clicked in his mind. "Jaz, I thought you were going to Philly to get to your dad."

"Oh hush, Frank," said his wife, Mary. "Not everyone has a great home life like we did, but that doesn't mean she has no father. Right, sweetie?" Although she sounded innocent as pie, Frank caught the note of alarm in his wife's voice. He'd known her long enough to know when her intuition was telling her something she didn't want to hear. He glanced at the rifles and saw Jed doing the same.

* * *

Jaz wouldn't look them in the eyes. Of course she had lied to them, but then she had gone and let her guard down. They were nice people, but it was still a mistake. She opened her mouth to lie, smiling, but then thought better of it. This wasn't a time to smile. Right-O, time to cowboy up.

"Listen, peeps, I really am going to Philly, but my dad's not there. I don't have a dad anymore. Most people look at you funny if you say that, so I lied. But the truth is worse. I got snatched up by some hickerbillies and they want your stuff. They sent me in here to get you to trust me. Tonight I was supposed to signal them, and they'd sneak in and take your stuff."

Amber growled at her, interrupting, "You did *what?* You little bitch, I'll—"

Jaz cut her off, raising her voice over Amber's low growl. "*Listen to me.* I can't do it. I don't want anything to happen to your kids, or you peeps. There's only three of 'em, and there's six of you. You got guns, too. Maybe we can, I don't know, trick them somehow?" It felt good doing the right thing, and Jaz smiled brightly for once, eager at the thought of turning it around on those stupid rednecks. "Yeah, and maybe I can join you guys? We can take *their stuff*, for once, and then just bounce out. Please," she begged.

Amber paused, and then she grinned, too, and for the first time in years, Jaz saw light at the end of the tunnel.

* * *

Frank froze, and a shiver ran from the base of his spine up to his scalp. This girl had come to harm his family but then warned them. Obviously, she couldn't be trusted, yet she was the only one who knew where the three gunmen were and what their plan was. He frowned as he realized his options were limited. "Okay, then. How were you to signal them, and what was their plan? Time for straight talk, girl. You're in it with us now, so lay it out."

Jaz nodded. "Well, after everyone went to sleep I was to come back out and get the fire going. If anyone asked, I was to say I couldn't sleep. They will come creeping after they see the fire, and blast everyone in the tents while they slept."

"And if we hadn't let you in, what would have happened then?"

"Plan B. They circle the camp and snipe the men first, then the women."

Frank saw Mary's face scrunch up in a frown. He hated it when his wife made that face—her plump, rosy cheeks were made for smiling. "Not to worry, then. We'll go along with the plan. You'll light the fire, Jaz, but when they come into the tents, they'll find three of us armed and waiting in each tent, rather than the sleeping sheep they were looking for. It's the best I can come up with."

Michael nodded slowly. "Yeah... It'll work. Has to work. One change, though. These guys are POGs—they have no experience that I can see. Their plan is wonky and lazy. So, I'll go outside the wire and wait for 'em. When they creep in I'll hit any targets of opportunity I see and take out any runners. With any luck, they'll be FUGAZI in seconds."

"Fugazee?" repeated Frank questioningly.

"Yeah, *fucked up, got ambushed, zipped in.* Dead."

Frank shook his head with a grin. "Michael, you don't say a lot, but when you do talk you still don't say a lot. Too many tours, friend. So in English, you'll sneak out Ranger-style and shoot the bastards from another direction. Yes?"

Michael smirked. "More or less."

"Okay then. Michael, get us set up in the tents and assign some guns. Don't worry about who owns what—we'll worry about that in the morning." He stood, stretched, and they set about getting ready for an eventful night.

* * *

SSgt Taggart watched as the lead vehicles darted in and out of the dead cars along Goshen Road north of Edgemont, PA. He hated taking these side roads, but the Lt. had decided it best not to go through West Chester, so they bypassed it and were now heading east along a rural road toward Highway 252, then to the 30, then north on I-476. Bah.

The soldier next to him who was driving said, "I sure hope the Lt. knows what he's doing, taking us on these middle of nowhere roads."

Taggart inwardly grinned but forced his face into a mask of displeasure. "Lock it up, Spec. If he says we take these roads, we do it. And make no mistake, Lt. Dunham is no ninety-day-wonder fresh from whatever petri dish breeds Butter Bars. He did a tour you don't have ribbon for, and has the salad to prove it."

In fact, Taggart thought, Dunham had lots of "salad," or ribbons and medals, and he was smart. Smart enough to query Taggart on a lot of things, yet tough enough to make his own decisions afterward. That being the case, Taggart was content to follow orders, not that he would ever refuse 'em.

He made a mental note to do the rounds among the men that night—the soldiers, he corrected himself—to bolster morale, or at least to enforce a bit of respect for the rank structure around here. A public chat with the Lt. about his tour in the Sandbox ought to do just fine.

SSgt Taggart's thoughts were interrupted when the vehicle in front of them slammed on its brakes, forcing his Hummer to an abrupt halt, as well. Even before they came to a full stop, he jumped out of the vehicle with his rifle and raced ahead, followed by every man and woman in the unit. He looked around as he went to make sure the soldiers fanned out and moved by pairs, just like they'd trained, but he needn't have worried.

He brought his attention back to the scene ahead as he ran between cars and stopped Hummers until he reached the lead vehicle. Just ahead of that, he saw soldiers standing over a woman lying on the roadway, pointing their rifles at her and commanding her to roll over. He let them get her into a safe position out of the roadway and on her belly, arms out with palms up, before inserting himself into the scene.

"What's the SITREP?" he barked as he walked casually up to the soldiers.

"Single civilian female nearly got her ticket punched by a Hummer, Sarge. She was walking in the middle of the road as we came barreling through. No collision, she jumped out of the way in time."

Taggart looked more closely at the civilian. She was in

her early thirties, brunette with shoulder-length hair in a ponytail. She was attractive enough, average height, and looked more fit than most civilians. She wore loose-fitting brown canvas pants, hiking boots, a black tee shirt under an unbuttoned blue flannel, with a gray a zip-up hoodie tied around her waist. Utterly sensible.

He spent about half a minute patting her down, and easily found her revolver and knife, which he handed to a soldier. Then, "Alright, ma'am. You can get up now. Are you injured?"

The woman stood, looking a bit shaky, and dusted herself off. "Thank you, sir. I'm not injured, just embarrassed. What the hell are you guys doing out here? I could have been killed," she demanded, face carefully blank.

"I'm SSgt. Taggart, ma'am. I'm glad you're okay. You shouldn't be out here alone. Things are getting... dicey out there, already." Turning to a soldier, he said, "Get the lady some coffee and a bite."

"I'm Cassandra," she replied. "Thanks, I could use a cup 'o joe. And things being dicey is the reason I'm out here, instead of on the main roads. I'm headed to Chesterbrook to get my kids and my mom, then heading out towards Lancaster. I have property north of there." She grinned, and said, "Satisfied?"

Taggart nodded. "Soldier, spread the word—chow time." He turned back to Cassy. "Cassandra, let's get some real food in you and talk about what's out there." Because he'd be damned if he'd pass up a chance for some intel about what they were headed toward.

* * *

Cassy was more than happy to tell them everything she knew. She even pointed out on the map everything she could

DARK NEW WORLD   91

think of, and though most of it had to be useless to the soldiers, their sergeant nodded at each thing she said and took careful notes. After a half hour, she'd told them all she knew, between bites of MREs. Then she said, "So, your turn. What the hell is going on out there?"

SSgt. Taggart frowned at her. "A lot I can't tell you, and a lot we don't know. The short version of what we *do* know and can share is this: One or more EMPs fried everything electronic in North America, and New York City is going to be attacked if it hasn't been already. We had a handful of Humvees that are older, and had been shielded against EMPs, and our orders are to get to New York ASAP. Small units are Sneaky Pete into the city from all over the East Coast region. We have some shielded radios, but the range is short so we are out of touch until we get closer. Meaning, I don't have a lot of actual knowledge about the country's SITREP."

Which also meant, Cassy noted to herself, that these soldiers got orders to move out *before* the lights went out... Interesting, and scary. She fought to keep her face expressionless.

"Anyway," Taggart continued, "Lancaster's FUBAR. Avoid it if you can, when you get your family. But ma'am, there's the same situation in every city we've been through. I don't feel right about leaving you out here. There might be a refugee camp between here and New York if you want to come with us. Get a ride, get to safety. They might even be able to send someone out to get your family."

Cassy didn't think that was very likely. "Thanks, but no thanks. I'm getting to my family first, then we'll decide what to do, together."

Taggart shrugged. "Can't say I blame you. But help a poor soldier sleep at night, and promise me you'll stay off the damn roads from now on. Even if you don't get run over, there's a lot of people wandering around following these roads, hoping one place is better than the last. They're hungry and desperate. Get me?"

She did, and finished eating while the sergeant got his soldiers ready. Ten minutes later, the unit of soldiers was prepared to move on. Cassy thanked them for the four MREs and two full canteens they'd given her along with her pistol back and waved as they left. She watched them go and wondered if she'd made the right decision. Could she actually get to her family? Would they all then get to her homestead in time, even if she did find them in all this mess? No right answers, only decisions. She sighed and shrugged her shoulders as she turned to continue on in the opposite direction as the soldiers.

But then she froze. There was a faint roar that she could barely make out. As she paused to listen, however, the roaring got louder and it dawned on her that what she heard was a jet engine. She looked up hoping to see an airliner but then realized the long odds on that happening. A thrill went up her spine as she realized it had to be military aircraft. Yeah, now Uncle Sam had some tools to throw at the Big Apple, she thought excitedly.

Three jets, clearly fighter craft, streaked overhead at a pretty good height but were going fairly slowly following a course roughly parallel to the roadway. Two of the jets continued onward, but one banked steeply to the right. Following it with her eyes, Cass caught sight of the soldiers. They frantically drove the Humvees right into the road's shoulders, and she could see even from that distance that they scrambled out of the vehicles and to scatter along the sides of the road in the foliage. In seconds, she could not see one soldier. It occurred to her that she ought to follow their lead, and sprinted off the road, sliding into cover behind a thick bush. But why would they hide from their own planes?

The question was quickly answered. As the lone jet turned around, she could see that it looked nothing like any American fighter she had seen. The angles were wrong, the coloration was wrong. She couldn't see the "logo" on it, but it was definitely not the American star.

Cassy watched with horror as the fighter screamed inbound, low and menacing, and she heard a distinct buzzing noise. Several of the dead cars on the road, along with two Hummers, exploded into bright balls of fire rising into the air, and she realized the fighter had used its guns to strafe the roadway. Once it flew past the carnage it banked steeply, and in moments, it faded into the distance, no doubt on its way to catch up to the other two.

As the soldiers arose from their hiding places, she heard faint shouting, and the soldiers were a hornet's nest of activity. Unsure whether the plane would return, and with no skills to help the soldiers, Cassy decided it was time to get the hell out of there. And, by God, she would stay off the damned roads.

- 17 -

1200 HOURS - ZERO DAY +3

MANDY STOOD IN the kitchen with Brianna and Aidan, staring at the pantry. All that remained were three cans of chili, a can of corn, and two English muffins. Once those were gone, they would all be down to flour, cornmeal, and vinegar. She fought back tears, and muttered, "I should have gone shopping before you got here. I knew I shouldn't have waited until tomorrow. There was no tomorrow..."

"Yeah, probably should have," said Brianna, a frown etched on her face. "I don't want chili, Grandma."

Aidan slipped his arm around Mandy's hip, as high as he could comfortably reach, Mandy knew. "It's okay, Grandma. You aren't psychotic."

"Psychic, dear. I'm not psychic."

"Oh yeah," said Aidan. "Well, you're not psychotic either."

Brianna let out a heavy sigh. "Shut up, butthead."

Mandy had to chuckle despite herself. "You two kids, what will I do with you," she grinned.

Then she, too, let out a sigh as she looked at the cans of chili. She was with Brianna on this one—chili was not her favorite. She mostly bought it for Aidan, who could eat the stuff twice a day and three times on Sunday. She suspected he just wanted gas, to bother Brianna. Those two kids...

"Well, lunch today is whole-kernel golden corn in a Roux reduction plated over Muffin du English," Mandy said, and the kids groaned.

"God, Grandma," said Brianna as she rolled her eyes, "don't try to French it up, it's corn and flour over stale muffins."

Aidan said in a breathless whisper, "I wish mom was here."

And Mandy could only agree though she didn't respond. Instead, she reached for the flour.

After lunch, Mandy was still hungry. She knew the grandkids had to be hungry as well, but there was nothing for it. They had to make it last until Cassy got there, and that was that. Hungry times were ahead for everyone, she knew.

She looked around the table at the kids. Brianna had her elbows on the table—and Mandy let it slide—with her face in her hands, and none of her usual banter. Aidan, hands in his lap, slouched over the table, plate inches from his face. Altogether, Mandy thought, it was a melancholy scene.

Aidan finally spoke. "Grandma, are we gonna starve? I don't want to starve. I've never been sooo hungry." He hadn't moved from his perch over his plate.

Brianna let out a quiet sob, and Mandy realized her granddaughter was crying into her hands, trying to hide her tears. God be merciful, but it was time to buck up, Mandy decided. Fake it 'til you make it, her daughter would say, and she could almost hear Cassy's voice as the thought went through her mind.

"That's it. Stop this, kids. We are *not going to die*. Your mom is on her way, and you both know she can find food enough for everyone. We may be hungry, and we may hate what little we do eat, but we aren't going to starve. In fact, Aidan—I want you to go up to the attic and look for anything useful. Wire, fishing line, anything. Check every box. We're going to do this ourselves until your mother gets here."

Mandy said it with gusto, resounding with confidence. But it was confidence she didn't feel. It would just give the boy something to do to feel useful, to feel like they were *doing something* about the situation. Brianna needed that too, she knew. So she continued, "Bri, I have a special task for you. I want you to go into the yard, and get out to the shed. Find hammers, hatchets, knives. There's a tent out there, and sleeping bags; get those, too. And fetch the tackle box out of there."

Brianna lifted her head at last and put on a half-hearted smile. "Okay, Grandma. Got a plan?"

"I sure do, kids. It may not be a great plan, but it's something, at least. Now get going, and accomplish the mission!"

The kids said in unison, "Accomplish the mission, aye aye, Grandma."

It might have been only half-hearted, but at least Mandy had them all on the same page, focused on something other than the growling pit of hunger in their bellies. It was a start. It was *something*. Mandy nodded, dismissing them.

But before the kids got going, in the distance, Mandy felt as much as heard a series of deep *whump, whump, whump* noises. Some part of her recognized they were explosions. Seconds later, she heard the faint noise of jet engines, far away or high above. All three looked at each other, eyes wide. Mandy felt hunger give way to fear, and she barely heard Brianna begin to cry again. Perhaps they'd need that tent sooner than she'd thought.

* * *

Tyrel Alexander slowly woke to the sound of his stomach growling. His head felt as if a hammer was keeping a steady beat on his skull, and the fading light coming through the curtained windows of his hotel room was a blinding laser of pain. "Goddamn hangover," he muttered as he got to his feet, struggling to stay balanced. He hated this part of drinking. Waking up still drunk without the buzz, but with all the physical effects... Well, it sucked. A lot.

He staggered to the bathroom and relieved himself, then flushed the toilet. He turned to the sink and grabbed the cheap plastic cup next to it, and tore off the wrapper. He put the cup under the faucet, but turning the handle, nothing came out. His mouth was full of cotton and his tongue felt about two sizes two big. Almost desperately, he turned the shower on. Again, no water came out. "What the hell?"

He started to swing his fist at the mirror in frustration but stopped short. He'd have to pay for it if he broke it. So he stood still for a long moment, slowly counting to ten. His mind started working through the boozy fog. Okay, if the power went out, then there'd be nothing to pump water, right? But the hotel had to have water tanks on the roof. Could they be dry already? No way, he thought. But then another thought struck him. What day was it? Could he have been blind drunk longer than he'd thought?

A sudden bout of nausea had him vomiting in the toilet for several minutes. Shaking and ashen, he stood and wiped the dribbles off his mouth and chin with his sleeve, then flushed. Again, nothing happened. He realized the tank must not have refilled. Ugh, no running water.

Ty managed to get his shoes on, screw the socks, and wobbled his way to the door. Vending machines were downstairs... He came out of his room, made his way to the stairwell, and headed to the first floor. Emerging, he saw that the lobby was dark, and there were no people anywhere he could see. "What the hell?" he said once again as his mind fought to make sense of what he saw.

Then he looked around more carefully. He still found no people, and all the vending machines were overturned and broken open. The little snack shelves were bare. Same with the soda machine.

A voice behind him said, "Nothing in those, friend."

Ty spun around by reflex, then wobbled in place trying to stay upright as the room continued to spin long after he had stopped turning. He fought down another bout of nausea, then squinted to see who had spoken. Before him stood two men and a woman, all wearing backpacks.

One of the men, the shorter one, had a shotgun in one hand with the barrel resting on his shoulder. "You look like shit," he commented.

"Yeah," croaked Ty, his dry throat protesting against the effort, "I been on a bender since the lights went out. Got any water? I'm dying for a drink of something besides whiskey."

The woman laughed. "We sure do. Lots of water. What do you have to trade?" As she said that, she unslung her backpack and pulled out a plastic water bottle.

"Trade? Nothing, I guess. But I need some water." He paused and looked at the three others, but they were making no move to hand over the water bottle. "Well? Give me some water, man. I'm thirsty."

"No way," said the woman. "You either trade or go screw yourself." She put the bottle back in her pack and slung it over one shoulder.

An ember of alcohol-inspired anger flared up within him. Still not thinking clearly, he knew only that he *needed that water*. His body cried out for it, and vaguely Ty knew that he really did need it, and right now. "Dammit, give me the water," he cursed at them, clenching his fists. Without realizing it, he took a step towards them. The situation changed dramatically in a heartbeat, then.

The taller man pulled a blade, and Ty saw that it was a survival-style knife. Like what Rambo might use, maybe, he thought. This guy was freakin' fruit loops if he thought pulling a knife would scare ol' Tyrel. Who would stab someone over a bottle of water, anyway? His anger grew. Words slightly slurred, he said, "Put that away and give me some water, or I'ma beat it outta you."

The shorter man laughed, and swung the barrel of the shotgun down to point at Ty. "No way, coz. Get out or get down, you feel me?"

Ty stopped short. "You want to shoot a man over *water*? What the hell is the matter with you people? Give me a bottle and just go get more, you assholes," he shouted.

"Ain't no more, fool," said the larger man.

Ty saw the woman pull out a pistol though she didn't aim it at him, yet. Then it reached through the fuzz in his brain that something truly terrible had to have happened for there to be no more food or water. Something big enough to keep the trucks from just bringing more, like they always did. And if the trucks weren't coming, then help wasn't on its way. Cass had been right to leave while she could. The thought was bitter, and panic rose inside him.

"You selfish bastards," he yelled, now panicked beyond reason. "You give me some damn water. I need it, and you can either kill me with those guns or you can kill me by walking away. Well, I'm not letting you just walk away. What kind of monsters are you?"

Tyrel clenched his fists and darted towards them. But, still drunk, his foot caught on the corner of a lobby couch and he tumbled head-first into the glass table, shattering it. He felt the glass slicing him along his face, neck, arms... The pain shot through him and drove away the fog of booze. He was going to bleed out if he didn't get help, he realized.

"Shit! Call 911. Someone do something," he cried out at the other three as he slowly stood. He could feel the warmth of blood seeping into his clothes, and hear its patter-patter as it dripped onto the floor.

The other three had looks of surprise on their faces, with the woman's mouth agape. She snapped her mouth shut and shook her head as though clearing a bad nightmare, then looked away from Ty. She stepped behind the shorter man, resting her head on his shoulder.

"Seriously," Ty said, now begging. "Someone help me!"

The larger man approached him but stayed out of lunging distance. "Sorry, coz. Nothing anyone can do for you now. Look."

Tyrel looked down and saw a large chunk of glass protruding from his stomach, high and to the left. "But, you can fix it, right? Please, you gotta try. You can't leave me like this, I'll *die*."

The man looked away, briefly, and said, "You gonna die now anyhow, man, slow and painful. That what you want?"

Tyrel couldn't understand. Why weren't they helping him? Why wouldn't they call 911, or get a towel, or something? Anything. "Hell no, I don't want to die like this. So goddammit, do something."

Tyrel watched the other man intently, adrenaline focusing his view until that was all he could see. And the other man nodded. Hallelujah, at last, they were going to do something to help him. Bastards. But the tall man didn't move. What the crap was this? "Well? Do it," he screamed.

The man looked Ty in the eyes. "I really am sorry," he said.

With one swift motion, Ty watched as the pistol came up. He saw right down the barrel. He began to protest, to open his mouth to scream, but before he could there was a bright flash and a loud bang.

And then only darkness.

* * *

Ethan Mitchel gripped the HAM radio mic so tightly that his knuckles were white. "Dark Ryder to Watcher One, say again, please."

The speaker crackled. "I said, a guy in Philly reports that people are already killing one another for food."

"Holy Batshit, fatman," Ethan muttered. It was his favorite intentional misquote though he could never remember where he'd heard it first. Clicking the mic, he said, "So it has really come to that. You safe where you're holed up, Watcher?"

"Yeah, thanks for asking, Ryder. I'm well-stocked and well-protected. You?"

"Don't worry about me, Watcher. I'll be fine."

"So, I heard the same thing about D.C. and Charlotte. Any confirmation, there?"

"News to me. But you know, with no food network it's going to be the same everywhere."

"Stay low and stay hid, Dark Ryder."

"Right. Oh, and this just in: I guess the civilians in New York are fighting back against the 'vaders. Word has it the gangs are the only sorta-kinda government, and they're organizing resistance."

"Well, that is good news. I've heard it's the same in Orlando, but they got the OpFor, or the bad guys I mean, hemmed up. The invaders control just about everything, but only when they got a squad of men on site. Otherwise, it's open season on 'em. But they're mowing down civilians in retribution."

Ethan frowned, but really, how could it be otherwise?

102   JJ HOLDEN & HENRY GENE FOSTER

And every person they executed was one less mouth fighting for what little food remained. He felt dirty for thinking that.

A deep voice came over the radio, and Ethan recognized his old "friend" PinkToes' voice. "Dark Ryder, hey, more info. I just got three-way confirmation that outside the cities, the Army is rounding up supplies from people. Requisitioning it. And if they resist, people are getting shot for hoarding under this Martial Law rule."

"Shit," replied Ethan, not worried about FCC rules anymore. "If you go topside, keep low, PinkToes."

"Yeah, you too. I'm out, talk to you later. Keep your ears on."

* * *

Ethan sat at a desk staring at the huge wall map. It was covered in green pins where he'd heard rumors of U.S. troop activity, and it was pretty clear they were almost all on path to New York City. Maybe Uncle Sam hoped to make the fight so costly that the enemy would give up. Yeah, right... Whoever was invading, they weren't going anywhere anytime soon. Rumors still floated around that it was the Koreans, or the Chinese, or the Iranians, or the Russians, but no one could say for sure. None of his radiohead contacts had seen, let alone captured, an enemy soldier to question, so for now it remained a favorite topic of conjecture on the HAM circuit.

Crap, with people *killing one another* for their next meal, and the government looting its own citizens to try to keep throwing troops at New York, it seemed silly to worry about who was responsible. Of course, if Uncle Sam found out who had done this to us, they'd probably launch nukes and that would be bad for everyone about a half hour later when the enemy's answer came back. Assuming the U.S. still *could* launch, but he had to imagine they could. Shielded

ICBMs and submarines didn't care about EMPs.

For hours, Ethan paced his bunker waiting for the radio to crackle. Boredom and fear were a bad combo, he thought, and eventually he decided he had to stretch his legs. It became an overwhelming obsession, and he fought it for an hour before slapping on his holstered pistol. He climbed up the steel ladder at the north end of the bunker, up and up, eventually coming to a thick metal hatch with a circular handle on each side. He glanced at monitors mounted on the walls all around the door above his head, but they showed no movement, no thermal activity.

Ethan spun the inside handle and slowly opened the hatch above him, revealing the low light of dusk. He crawled out of the tube, then gripped the fake rock that covered the outside of the door and swung it closed. He looked around to make sure no one was present and moved out cautiously. He was only up here for a walk, he reminded himself, just so he wouldn't go batshit crazy down there. Thank God he wasn't claustrophobic, he told himself.

The hatch was in the back half of the nearly three-quarters of an acre property his small house sat on, and the bunker had been put in first. After the bunker went in, he'd let the property sit vacant for a year before putting the small two-bedroom home on it; long enough for the neighbors to forget the previous unusual construction. He'd told the neighbors he bought the property from a crazy old guy who never got around to building the basement he'd wanted, and they believed him.

Then Ethan made sure no one really was in his small house before he went inside. All was as it had been, except the refrigerator and all the cabinet and pantry doors were open. Everything edible was gone, of course. He walked to the bay window in his living room and sat on an ottoman. He just looked and looked. All was silent. Nothing moved, save a couple of cats that had been wily enough to escape human attention. The town was dead, without a shot being fired by the enemy. As he watched the sun set over the neighborhood, Ethan's thoughts were sad and somber.

"The cost of freedom is always high, but Americans have always paid it. And one path we shall never choose, and that is the path of surrender, or submission," he muttered. With heart aching, he added, "God help us all."

- 18 -

2100 HOURS - ZERO DAY +3

AS THE SUN finished setting, Frank sat with the other adults around the fire, as they did every night after the kids had gone to bed inside the tents, but no one seemed much into talking. Michael insisted they couldn't vary from routine, not with unknown gunmen possibly watching every move, so they sat together as usual.

Of them all, Jaz seemed the most frightened. Frank thought about how difficult it must be for the young woman to finally make some sort of stand. She'd shared a bit of her past, including what happened with the bastards who sent her into their camp. Frank knew she'd had to face down some mighty powerful demons to open up to his people like that. Nor could he blame her for taking that woman's backpack, whoever she'd been. Jaz was alone with nowhere to go. The woman at least had more food and real shelter close by. But Jaz was sure enough one weird little bundle of self-sufficiency and total, abject passive acceptance... Too young, really, to know herself or where she would draw her personal lines.

"Why do you think they sent Jaz in here," Michael asked,

breaking into Frank's thoughts. "I mean, if it had been me I would have just waited until right before dawn to creep in when I knew everyone would be sawing logs. Never mind sending Jaz in here. That only introduced a wildcard."

Frank knew Michael was thinking things through aloud, not asking a real question. Hell, Michael could answer that question better than anyone else in camp—he was the only one who had served. Frank had heard some stories of the things he'd done in Iraq and Afghanistan.

Nonetheless, Frank offered a suggestion. "Maybe they're just testing her. Seeing if she's really one of them. I gather she was pretty convincing," he said delicately. "I'd want to know, if it was me."

Jasmine stared at the fire without replying.

Michael shrugged. "Maybe. I have to remember they likely don't have training, so that could well be. More likely from my point of view would be that she's the recon, gathering intel. What guns are here, who's in what tent, what would be the best stuff to take if they wanted to hit and run instead of hanging around to do inventory."

That seemed to get Jaz's attention. She finally raised her gaze from the fire and shook her head, as though coming out of a dream. Or a nightmare. "Maybe, yeah. They did ask me to look for things that are useful and easy to carry, especially guns and ammo."

Frank didn't pay much attention to the rest of the conversation, which wandered onto other subjects. He sat silently, his head on the coming danger, on praying for his family that God might see them all through, and wondering how his own personal lines might change after tonight. But then, Frank was always the quiet one of the bunch.

* * *

Jaz sat by the fire, slowly adding logs to build it up. She was tense and alert, and she had no problem admitting to herself that she'd gone way beyond terrified. An hour ago Frank and Amber had play-acted an argument just outside of camp, complete with lots of pointing at Jaz, and then both had stormed into their respective tents. Jaz knew that was just for the benefit of anyone watching them, a distraction that allowed Michael to fade away. She didn't know where he was now, and hadn't seen or heard him leaving. Somewhere out there was Michael with a high-powered deer rifle, watching over them all. Frank and his wife were in one tent; Jed, Amber, and Tiffany were in the other. They had split the kids between the two. All was as ready as it could be, she thought as she fed another small log to the fire.

Jaz heard the faint crack of a branch or twig breaking from somewhere behind her. She turned to look, but could see nothing outside the ring of light from the fire. She sat like that for a minute, listening, but heard nothing else and turned back to the fire. She forced herself to act calm, but she had a knot of fear in her gut so strong that she felt like throwing up.

When a voice whispered behind her, she nearly jumped to her feet. "You done good, Jaz," said the man behind her. "Once we finish 'em off, you'll point out the stuff we need to take."

Jaz nodded curtly, hardly daring to move.

Her former captors moved in pairs to the tents; at each entry, one man drew a knife while the other readied his gun. One man then held out a finger, then two, then a third. After that, everything happened so fast she hardly knew it had started before it was done.

At each tent, the man with the knife slipped through the doorway. Two shots rang out on top of each other, and someone screamed. A half-second later, the man with the gun outside Frank's tent crumpled, his head seeming to explode. The other gunman turned, and then he collapsed just as the report from the first shot reached Jaz's ears. A moment later the *crack* of the second shot reached her. Somewhere out there, Michael blew a whistle, its shrill note startling a very wound-up Jaz.

Frank and the others in camp emerged from the tents, dragging bodies out. Frank looked pale even in the dim light of the fire, and the kids cried loudly. As Jaz sat on her log bench, still so frozen in fear her stomach churned, Jed turned to face her and smiled. Blood, not his own, had splattered over Jed's face, and a bit of what looked to be skull fragment stuck out from within his short beard.

Jasmine leaned over and puked.

- 19 -

0600 HOURS - ZERO DAY +4

CASSY AWOKE EARLY to the sounds of birds chirping. Her first thought was that she should already be with her kids, quickly followed by a flood of anger at the delays. She sat up and rubbed her eyes, picked up a rock and threw it at one of the damn birds. She missed it completely. Yes, it would be one of those days, she thought, and climbed out of her makeshift "bed." But then she stopped and took a deep breath. She would reach her mother's place that evening if she could get through the little towns about five miles north along Highway 30.

She'd come as far as something called the "Kirkwood Preserve" before making camp the night before, but had not yet entered it. In the light of morning, she saw that it was a vast open park, with only a tree or two here and there for cover. The rest was completely exposed. Before doing anything else, she nibbled on an MRE the poor soldiers had given her and then gathered up her things.

Some of the terrain was quite steep, at least on the north end of the preserve where she'd made camp. To get a better view, she walked up a hill. At the top, she let out a low whistle. The view was gorgeous, alright, but the preserve was curiously devoid of anything but scattered trees. The dense woods she had camped in ended abruptly at a fence line.

Some preserve, she smirked. Preserving what, grass? But she was glad she had decided to camp outside of it, as she would not have found much cover from the wind and cold there. Her tiny fire would have been seen for a great distance, despite using a Dakota Fire Hole—a nearly smokeless fire. It was a trick she'd learned from one of her many books, digging a small tunnel and feeding sticks in one end so the fire would jet through to emerge out the other. Sort of like a prehistorical rocket stove, she laughed when she first realized how it worked. As her mom had said so often, the more things change, the more they stay the same.

A small tuft of dirt disappeared only feet from her, and she stared at the spot trying to make sense of it. A moment later she heard the report of a gunshot. Cassy dropped to her belly and slid back down the hill a couple feet. As she did so, her mind raced. The shot wasn't loud enough to be close, nor faint enough to be distant. In a way, that only put her in more danger because she couldn't do much with her little pistol beyond about thirty yards, yet they would be close enough to see anything she did. It also meant whoever had fired that shot used a rifle, and that was just bad news for her.

Cassy struggled to calm down, and then forced herself to peek over the crest to see where the threat was though her fear told her to slide down the hill and run into the woods. No, they had seen her and must still be a ways away. It was more important to see what she was up against, she decided. Fighting down her fear, she crawled back up to the crest of the hill to peer over.

What she saw made her blood run cold. Three people on horseback, armed with rifles, rode in her direction hell-bent for leather. With those rifles, if they caught her in the open, she was done for. Her panic took over and, frantic, she slid down the hill, then sprinted toward the woods. Ten yards. Five yards. Just as she passed through the sharp edge of the tree line, another shot rang out and a bullet struck a tree only a foot to her right.

Cassy kept running, legs pumping and lungs beginning to burn. Her only hope, she knew, was to lose them as they tried to follow her into the woods, at least long enough to find a place to hide. If they rode in after her, they must slow down, and if they dismounted it gave her precious time.

As Cassy ran deeper into the woody cover, she heard the people behind her shouting, but couldn't hear the words over the beating hooves of the horses. But then the hoof beats vanished, and she rejoiced when she realized they must have dismounted. She had a head start and fear on her side... Surely they could never catch her now.

Cassy continued running for what seemed an hour, her heartbeat thundering in her ears. When she reached the limit of her endurance, she found a tall tree where the soil had eroded to leave a woody cave beneath heavy, exposed roots. It was large enough to hide her, she saw, and, grabbing a new-fallen branch, she squirmed into the opening, scraping up soil with the branch to attempt a bit of camouflage. She didn't have time for a proper job of it and hoped her pursuers would be too rushed to notice her. She was too exhausted to continue anyway and cursed herself for not being in better shape *before* she needed to run from armed marauders.

She pulled out her pistol, and prayed under her breath, "I will fear no evil..."

* * *

Peter Ixin cursed again. The woman had to be a spy from one of the towns to the east, along I-476. He felt bad for those people, or anyone in a suburb. As the hunger spread, the cities were emptying right into the 'burbs, bringing looting and chaos in their wake.

White Stag Farms had brokered something of a coalition in the more rural areas around the farm, the area between West Chester in the west and Upper Darby in the east. They traded from their stockpiles of food for hired guns and hired hands. Even so, with pressure from the hungry people coming from every direction, he had his hands full convincing would-be looters to find somewhere else to loot.

These damn spies made that task near impossible, looking for weaknesses or a way through the homesteads and forests and into the agricultural heartland of White Stag's controlled area. Small bands of riders like his own were tasked to seek out and find such spies, or warn of larger incursions incoming if and when those came. And they surely would come in force once hunger outweighed risk.

Peter wasn't sure they could hold off the masses of people who must be on their way, but he'd be damned if he would give up his home, his friends, his neighbors. Not without a fight. He grew up right there near White Stag Farms, and he would die to protect it if necessary. Where else would he go, anyway? The shit was not just in Philadelphia. It was everywhere, all around them.

And this bitch was screwing up his program. She'd almost stumbled into their backup supply camp in Kirkwood Preserve's hilly terrain, and that just would not do. They'd run after the woman spy at full speed until he stopped hearing her crashing through the brush like a bull elephant. She was here, somewhere, hidden and possibly armed. He hoped not to lose another of his riders this time before they got the bitch.

He motioned to the man on his left, then the woman on his right. Left fist straight out to his side; spread out. Then left fist pumped straight up and down; hurry the hell up. Both flashed him the OK signal and moved away from him and ahead. They made moderate pace through the woods in that formation. Peter moved them methodically in an impromptu grid search. It could take hours to search every nook and cranny, but by God, he would find her, no matter what.

* * *

Cassy hid in her dirty tree-cave. About ten minutes in, she saw two of them pass by, spread well apart. One had passed quite closely and the other was to the south of her tree. She couldn't flee west, which was right back into the wide open preserve that got her into this mess in the first place. East were her hunters. She could go north, perhaps, but didn't know where the third hunter was. Likely, he was north of her... Very well, she would have to go south, away from her mother and her children. Dammit.

She was about ready to slide her way out of her hidey-hole when she heard noises to the east. Of course the hunters would be coming back right through her area, she mused. Nothing could be easy. Moving as little as possible, she peeked around the foliage she hid behind, searching for the marauders who hunted her.

There was one due east, a woman with a rifle who was far from quiet. To the north, she saw but did not hear the same man who had passed her before, going the other way. He was well ahead of the woman by perhaps as much as one hundred yards, and at least half that distance further north. No sign of the third marauder, she realized, and decided he must be a lot farther north of her. They must be going back and forth, which meant all she had to do was wait out the clumsy woman and then slide away to the south. She would be free, with her hunters none the wiser.

The need to wait, with her heart thundering and her vision narrowed from adrenaline, was excruciating. Every fiber of her being wanted to run, get away, before the other woman stumbled onto her. She calmed her breathing as best she could, and repeated in her mind over and over that she was hidden, she would not be found, she would escape. She would see her family again.

That did the trick, and slowly her heart rate slowed. Waiting became easier, and her thoughts wandered to scenes of her kids and other bits of a life well lived. Would her mother understand why it took Cassy so long to rescue them? Would she understand that the family's journey to Cassy's homestead would then be just as perilous as her journey so far?

The crack of a twig just outside the shelter made her freeze. Thoughts of family were gone in an instant.

* * *

Peter looked and saw that, to the south, the new scout was well behind him. She looked alert and had her rifle ready. She'd shown a bit of confusion when they first shifted grid north and then back to the west, but all in all she caught on quickly enough. She had to, he mused, because there weren't enough supplies to waste on slackers. His report on her would be favorable to keeping her in the growing little commune around White Stag Farms.

When he saw the girl freeze in place, he diverted his attention to her. She must have seen something, he realized, and quickly changed direction. As he tried to close the distance, he saw her aiming her rifle at a large bush. She had her eyes narrowed, trying to see something. Peter revised his opinion of her just a little.

"Thought I heard something," she whispered when Peter came close.

Peter nodded once, raised his rifle, and fired a round into the bush. A raccoon scurried out from under the bush like hell itself was after it, and Peter chuckled. "Listen, recruit. If you're sure none of your guys is behind that bush, when hunting a spy who might be armed and hiding in that bush... Well, feel free to waste a bullet rather than catching one. You can't defend the White Stag Farms coalition if you're dead, right?"

"No, sir." She frowned, disappointed in herself perhaps.

Peter smiled and put a hand on her shoulder. "I know we're hard pressed by the city people. Those Havertown Militia scum can be tough. We need you. So again—shoot first. We need every scout, defender, and warden we have. We can replace a bullet, but we can't replace you so easily. Got it?"

Peter then moved away, using hand signals to motion the other scout back into position, and the three moved out again.

* * *

Cassy nearly wet herself when she heard the shot, even though she could see it wasn't aimed at her. Paralyzed, she watched through the small gaps in camouflage as the silent-moving man laughed at the raccoon running for its life. He spoke with the woman briefly—and boy, wasn't that a big bit of information she overheard!—then moved north to pass out of her field of view. The woman stayed where she was and put hands to knees, gathering herself. Cassy was grateful—

she seemed inexperienced. Maybe a minute later, the woman moved on, trying to be quiet as she returned to her westward path.

But then, as she passed close by Cassy's hidey-hole, the woman stopped again. Cassy watched the woman listen intently, scanning her eyes side to side. The barrel of her rifle moved with her head, covering whatever she happened to be looking at. But after long seconds, she seemed satisfied nothing was amiss and walked on.

Cassy realized she'd been holding her breath since the woman stopped, and forced herself to take slow and steady breaths. Also, her arms were tired; she'd been holding the pistol forward in both hands, aiming at the woman. She allowed her arms to fall slowly.

She heard the sound of fabric on branches; her hoodie sleeve had caught on some twigs among her camouflaging branches. Her eyes darted to the marauder, maybe a dozen paces away, just as the woman's head—and rifle—swung towards the noise. Fuck getting shot, Cassy screamed in her head, panicking as the rifle barrel moved inexorably toward her.

A shot rang out. The marauder's head whipped back, blood spraying from the back of her head, and then she toppled over like a marionette with its strings cut.

Part of Cassy's mind noted that when people get shot, they didn't go flying like in the movies. It was more like a light switch turning off.

Then she remembered the other man, who couldn't be more than a hundred yards away, and leaped out of her hiding spot through the haphazard covering. Branches scratched at her face, her hands, her clothes, but they did not stop her. She dove for the woman's rifle and brought it to her shoulder, aiming in the direction the man had gone.

There! Just there. A movement in a bush by a tree. As

she fired there was a metallic *TING!* and she saw the marauder fall over like a tree toppling. She realized she'd dropped her pistol, and wasted a second that seemed a lifetime to find it and tuck it back into its holster. Without thinking, then, she spun on her heels and ran. Southward she went, flying through the forest as quickly as her legs would take her. She'd hit her second wind while resting in the hollow of the tree, and felt as though she'd never run so fast.

Seconds went by, then minutes. After twenty more minutes of running, she slowed to an easy jog but kept going. There was no way in hell she was going to stop until her damn legs fell off, she swore, dodging to and fro as the endless trees passed by.

* * *

Peter blinked a couple times. Even in the faint light of the forest, his head throbbed. He reached to his forehead and his hand came away bloody. Still a bit in shock, his mind reeled to connect all the events, to make sense of what just happened, but at first it was just a jumbled mess. Sitting up, he saw another scout approaching at a run, rifle at the ready. Good boy, he thought, the soldier in him recognizing the muscle memory his training had given the young man.

"Peter, are you hit, sir?" the other scout said. He whipped off his backpack, intent on pulling out the first aid kit.

Yeah, that'd help a gunshot wound to the noggin. "Stop. Breathe. Examine my skull. Am I shot? First things first, kid."

The young scout did as he was told, and after a second he moved Peter's hair around, looking for a wound. "No, sir. You have a cut to your skull above the hairline, sir. What happened?"

It was coming back to Peter, now. He'd heard a shot fired. It wasn't one of his scouts, wasn't a rifle report, so he'd turned to run toward the noise. He was about to careen around a bush when another shot had been fired. A rifle shot, that time. "The spy. She got hold of a rifle and fired at me, but it struck my weapon. I reckon it was my own barrel that gave me the cut. Go check on Amy while I get some pressure on this bitch," he ordered.

Gingerly, he took off his sweater. Then he folded it and placed it to his wound with a grimace of pain. He staggered towards where the shot had been fired and noted that his feet didn't seem to work right. Goddammit, a freakin' concussion? There was no way he could pursue the spy, not in this condition.

He stopped feeling sorry for himself when he came up to the young scout and saw him standing over Amy's body. Most of the back of her head was missing and her eyes would never see again, pretty as they had been. Peter let out a long, low growl of suppressed rage. "Kid, go get the horses and grab whatever's left of my rifle. We gotta get this young scout home, and make sure more scouts are sent out to look for this bitch."

The younger man ran off, but Peter didn't move. He only stood over Amy's corpse—he only barely knew her name—and swore he would avenge her death. She was defending *his* family as well as her own, *his* community, which she had become a part of. As soon as the vet stitched him up, he was damn sure going to ride out again, looking for revenge.

- 20 -

1000 HOURS - ZERO DAY +4

FRANK SWEATED AS he dragged a body away from the camp. At least a hundred yards, Michael had said. The ground was uneven, and the man was dead weight. Frank chuckled at the pun, wiping his brow, then put his back into the task again. Michael and Jed were nearby, struggling with their own loads. None of the men spoke, nor had anyone said much since the ambush. When the bodies were far enough away, in silence, they covered the bodies with leaves and fallen branches. It was the best the bastards would get, Michael had said, and Frank agreed wholeheartedly.

As they walked back into camp, Frank saw that Tiffany, Amber, and his wife Mary were salvaging as much as they could, cleaning blood off coolers and cookware. He didn't think they'd gone back into the tents yet—they'd refused since the ambush, and he couldn't blame them. Who wanted to sleep in a slaughterhouse with brains and guts splattered everywhere?

Frank saw that Jaz was still sitting where she had slept. He was worried about the girl; she hadn't moved or said anything since the attack began. Poor kid, he thought. The beautiful young woman had probably never seen anything more graphic than a school yard fight. She was city-soft, and she'd have to toughen up right quick to survive in this new world, but she'd clearly had enough "toughening" for one day. He hoped there wouldn't be more toughening any time soon.

He took in the others in the party at a glance; they still functioned, which was a relief. Whenever they passed Jaz, they patted her head or smiled encouragement if they caught her eye. The wives had stopped thinking of her as a gorgeous outsider endangering their marriages and had become doting maternal whirlwinds. Yep, Jaz was one of them now, alright. And Frank took care of his own, even if they weren't family by blood. He owed this young woman for saving his family from probable death, or worse.

He snapped out of his thoughts when he felt a hand on his shoulder. He looked over and saw Jed next to him, concern etched on his face.

"You still with us, big guy?" asked Jed, quietly enough that no one else would hear. "Last night was tough as gristle to swallow, but we got plenty left to do, Lord knows. Come join us at the fire—we got some jawin' to do, and it can't wait."

Frank nodded slowly and took a deep breath to clear his mind before following Jed toward the fire pit. "Alright, Jed. I'm here, what's on your mind?"

"Well, I reckon we're more interested in what's on your mind, Frank. We got ideas, but you always got a knack for shootin' holes in ideas that are 'all hat and no cattle.' "

"So what's on the table?" Frank replied, trying not to grin. Jed wasn't raised with a southern drawl as thick as the one he let on, but Frank thought it more amusing than irritating.

Jed ran his fingers through his hair, and said, "Well, me 'n Amber want to stay here. Figure out how to clean the tents, maybe put up some walls or somethin'. And Michael got it in his head to leave all this and tear off into the wild blue yonder, livin' off the land like hillbillies."

Frank glanced at Michael, who only shrugged. Short on words, that one, but apparently Jed had the gist of Michael's idea. "Alright, give me a minute," said Frank, and rubbed his temples. Sometimes it frustrated him that they always bugged him with their ideas, as though a simple mechanic with a green thumb knew anything more than they did.

Frank finally looked up, glancing from person to person. "Alright, here's what's what. Jed, your plan has no legs to stand on. We can't stay here. More people will be coming, and soon. We can't lay any roots here, and I don't want my kids to die defending land we can't lay use to."

Jed frowned but nodded. "That rings true, Frank. But wanderin' around aimless doesn't seem like a brilliant plan either..."

"I don't think we ought to do that, either. No offense to you, Michael," he said with a nod towards the other man, "You got skills none of us have, and I'm sure you can use 'em just fine. But the problem is right there—none of us have those skills. Not yet. I don't want to drag my wife and son away from here, only to die just as certain out there. We need a third option."

Frank looked around the group and saw them watching him expectantly. Damn it, he didn't ask to be any kind of leader, but Michael was young and full of testosterone, and Jed was a good man, but dull.

"Alright. What we need is this: we take what we can carry, especially guns and water, and head west away from

Philly and the hungry nightmare goin' on there right now. Find us a farm or something, either vacant or a place that can use some able bodies with guns. Earn our keep, and do some good for others in the process. It's both smart and the Christian thing to do, I think, though I'm no preacher."

Frank thought Jed was doubtful, which he expected, but Amber wore a smile. Good, Jed would go with what his wife wanted if he ever wanted peace again. Michael was no surprise; he nodded, face set in that way he always got when he talked about his missions in Iraq or wherever. Determination is what it was, and his own brand of honor. Tiffany only sat with her arm around Michael's waist, head on his shoulder. She'd go along with it.

Then he turned to his wife, but Mary looked back at him with eyes narrowed, lips pressed tightly together, which surprised him. "Alright hon, speak your piece."

"I'm with Jed," she said flatly. "We should stay." Frank couldn't hear any emotion in her voice, which meant she was scared. "We can't leave a perfectly good camp with fresh water, animals all around, just to take a chance some farmer yokel won't shoot us rather than hear us out. It isn't safe for Hunter."

"Don't bring our son into this like that, hon. You know very well I would never put him in danger. You think I'd send the boy up to the nearest looted homestead to ask pretty please, would you let all these extra mouths stay with you, Mr. Farmer? Hell no."

Mary's eyes flashed with anger, and she snapped her mouth shut so hard he could hear her teeth click together. She leaned forward and opened her mouth again, but was interrupted before she got started.

"Mary. Don't be stupid with Hunter's life," Michael said, slowly rising to his feet. "You're scared, we're all scared, but staying here will get your boy killed right quick. If not last night, then tomorrow night. Do you understand me? I *will not stay here* where every instinct I got says my kids and my wife aren't safe. You figure on staying here safe and sound without me? Without my guns, my traps, my tools?"

Mary sat rigidly and said nothing. To Frank's eye, she looked ready to start sobbing any minute from fear and anger.

Michael continued, "I swear to you, Mary, I will put my life in front of Hunter's. In front of yours. Any of us. I think we'd all do the same, given a second to think on it. Come with me, and we'll do Frank's thing. It's as solid a plan as we're going to get, Mary."

Mary let out her breath all at once, and Frank knew she'd been unconscious of holding it. He saw her shoulders sag a little. She would be on board, even if she didn't like it. Well and well, now they at least had a plan, which was better than sitting there waiting to die.

Frank coughed loudly, and heads turned toward him. "I must tell you all that I do know where to find a farm that will welcome us. We were invited though we declined to go at the time. No need to talk about who invited us," Frank said and locked eyes with Amber, then Michael. "But we'll be welcome there, and fed, with good people. That's all I have to say on it. I can't tell anyone what to do, but my family and I will go there. I hope you come with me."

Frank knew he'd have to talk to the others about where the homestead was. Cassy had only told him, and Frank didn't want that knowledge to die with him if something happened to him along the way. He was quickly learning just how abruptly a life could be snuffed out, and he pictured the man he'd killed inside his tent.

- 21 -

1200 HOURS - ZERO DAY +4

ETHAN MITCHEL LET out a long, slow breath. He pinched the bridge of his nose with one hand and drummed the fingers of the other on the desk. "Yeah, thanks for the intel, Watcher One," he said into the mic. "Dark Ryder out."

He stood, reached for a box of thumb tacks, and dug around for a while to find a color he hadn't already used for something else. Selecting eight white tacks, he methodically pushed them into the map. Two in upper New York. Two in western Pennsylvania. Two in Virginia. Connecticut. Vermont. And those were just the ones he knew about. These were the places where the enemy had bombed and sprayed vast areas of agricultural fields. Within hours, he had learned, anything leafy and green was dead, grains were wilting, and God only knew what it would do to the trees.

Ethan paced back and forth in his bunker, clenching and unclenching his fists, lips pressed tightly together. "Fuck!" he screamed, then stopped and took ten deep breaths. It didn't help any more than screaming had. Those bastards were busy destroying the only hope that nearly anyone within a hundred miles of New York City could survive. First the EMP destroyed the food distribution network, but he had reports that Uncle Sam was starting to organize horse and bicycle convoys to the smaller towns around New York; there was no way to bring in enough to make a dent in New York City's teeming hungry masses, and it had been written off.

But now the enemy was poisoning the food itself. Fuckers. He swore that if he ever saw these invaders, he'd go out in a blaze of glory, taking as many with him as he could. Of course, that would probably never happen. He wouldn't leave his bunker again any time soon, now that things were fully underway.

There was some good news, though. Watcher One, whoever he was in reality, had been sending good intel about recent events. While that included the news about poisoning or burning the food supply, it also included a large number of small US military units that were converging on the invasion areas, especially New York City. Somehow Watcher had concluded, or been told, that the units were coalescing, and were working with the Resistance. Ethan had little information about *them* except that they were doing some serious damage to the enemy, and that a group of leaders from various criminal organizations were directing them. Apparently they were really good at smuggling, hit and run, and avoiding being caught... Who would have thought that was useful, just five days ago?

As Ethan sat thinking, a loud beep sounded from one of his computers. "What the hell?" he said as he scrambled over, grabbed the mouse and sat with a hurried thump into the chair.

A desktop alert notified him that "an update was installed," and a spike of fear ran up his spine. He quickly found it; something called "AIR_RDEA." By reflex he moved the pointer to another application that would remove the thing, but a dialog box popped up first. A green cursor blinked in the box. Half a second later, a string of text appeared in the box.

ATTN: Dark Ryder - We know you're one of the 20s. They do not. Your service required. Ack.

"What the hell is this shit," Ethan muttered. How did they get a connection to his box? Well, his satphone was Bluetooth-enabled and had been set up as a satellite internet hotlink. His PC had Bluetooth connectivity. He hadn't turned any of that off after the EMP, as it wasn't a priority and didn't seem necessary. But somehow, someone had used the satphone connection to get into one of his PCs. True, this wasn't a big deal because he could shut the satphone off and bring up another computer, but it was damn upsetting.

Then he thought about just who might have the capacity and interest to contact him that way. Uncle Sam or the invaders led the short list, of course. Probably the good guys, but he couldn't be sure. It would be best to string along whoever was on the other end of the connection. Ethan wanted them to think Dark Ryder was a good little compliant sheeple.

Ack, you hacked Dark Ryder's box, DR responding. What service.

That's right, he mused, they hacked a box. Better be white hats or he'd sure as shit return the favor.

DR: retrieve attached txt file AIR_RDEA_411.txt

Ethan got up and verified his other four computers were powered down and unplugged their Ethernet cords, before returning to his chair. He pulled up an app to run a virtual machine, a sandbox; whoever was on the other end would see it was downloaded, but Ethan could access it without letting any unwelcome visitors run amok in the real system. *Click*, he downloaded the file and opened it.

It took Ethan quite a while to read through the lengthy text file, but from what he could see it appeared internally coherent, direct, and actionable. Holy crap, he thought, what the hell had he gotten involved in? A knot of anxiety formed deep in his gut and the walls felt a little tighter than they had before... He frowned, and replied at the terminal:

Ack receipt of file. Will respond in 24H after review. Go screw yourselves, btw.

Message sent, he pulled out his satphone and powered it down. He needed to think and had precious little time to do so.

* * *

Cassy needed to check her bearings. She stopped, pulled her map out of a cargo pocket and quickly narrowed down her location. She was just west of something called the Edgemont Country Club. Damn, she was farther from her family than when she'd met the soldiers on the road. Highway 30 lay ahead, less than a mile away. She could try to head north, skirting the east side of West Chester, but she ruled that out. The entire region would be unsafe, what with starving urbanites to the west and those farmer-scout-marauders to the east. No, she decided bitterly, she would have to go around West Chester's south end, before heading north again. It would add a couple days to her journey. Thankfully, she had MREs courtesy of Uncle Sam's finest, so she wouldn't have to slow to forage and hunt along the way.

As she folded up her map, images swept through her mind of the woman she shot. Oh sure, she had probably killed James and had definitely left him for dead, and did so happily, but James was a bad dude. He had lost any shred of civilized behavior before America's corpse had even cooled. That woman, though, had only been defending her home, doing what Cassy herself would have done. It was Cassy or the other woman, she knew, but she didn't feel any better about it. She shook her head to clear her mind and once again stuffed the terrible memories and feelings deep inside. That mental box was getting full to bursting, and Cassy thought she'd have a meltdown eventually. She just hoped it would happen *after* she found her kids.

Cassy took a good look around. Just west of her lay another preserve, and she was certainly not going to risk going into one of those again even if it had more trees than the last one. North looked great, but she didn't want to run into those scout-marauders again. Due south was the only option. From her vantage, it looked sparsely populated, which was good. Better yet, after about three miles it ran into a densely wooded area that then stretched off to the west well past West Chester, with only occasional residential areas to break it up. If she traveled quickly enough, she could be well into the woods by the time dusk arrived.

Alrighty, then—decision made.

* * *

Moving west for the last hour, Cassy paused to wipe sweat from her forehead. It was maybe about 3:00 p.m., she guessed, and she had made it to the woods without any new troubles. She had arrived at a tall, forested hill, and now decided to climb it for a good look around. If it looked promising, she'd camp there in the lee side, without a fire to draw attention to herself.

She scrambled up the side of the hill and was having a difficult time until she realized that she could grab on to the young trees that forested the hill and use them to pull herself up. Progress slowed but was safer and easier. After another twenty minutes, she made it to the top and found a pond. That struck her as odd until, from her new vantage, she saw that the hill was nearly circular. Man-made, then, but the pond made fresh water available and cemented her plan to camp there for the night.

Shortly, as the sun in its descent neared the horizon, the breeze shifted. She moved to the lee of the hill to shelter out of the wind and set about making a simple lean-to with branches and leaves. Some fresh boughs made a bed of sorts. Then she sat, letting out a sigh of relief to be off her sore feet and weary legs. It was pretty up there, she mused, gazing out over the southern view her camp gave her.

To the south, it looked mostly agricultural, interspersed with wooded areas. There was also a small village she figured had to be Glen Mills, judging by her map. Sure enough, she saw a school far to the south that must be Glen Mills Middle School, north of the village proper. She felt relieved to have been able to use landmarks and her map to fix her actual position. That would make the next stage of her journey safer, as she had a reliable way to avoid stumbling into any residential areas. Those would be terribly dangerous by now, especially to an outsider unfamiliar with the terrain.

Something bothered her all of a sudden. She shrank into her lean-to and looked around, but could see nothing that might have triggered her instincts so strongly. She sat still, listening and looking, but after perhaps thirty seconds she realized what was bothering her. She became aware of a faint, low hum in the distance. Airplanes, her mind made the leap. More than one. She listened carefully until she could tell from which direction the noise came: the planes were due east. Searching high and low, she spotted three dots low in the sky, moving fast.

As the dots approached, she saw that they were some sort of fighter craft. Not the jet fighters she had seen strafing the soldiers, but larger. Smaller than bombers or airliners but definitely jet powered. She watched as they banked to their left, shifting bearing to the southwest, and started to lose altitude.

The three large fighters—or whatever they were—leveled out at an altitude of maybe 1,000 feet, and continued to the southwest. The two outer planes then began spraying something, the spray spreading out into a thin, wide cloud that drifted down over what had to be farms. The third plane, in the center of the formation, launched rockets one after the other. She counted six rockets, which all went in different directions before striking various buildings that looked small from her vantage, but might have been grain silos or processing plants. Once out of spray and rockets, the three planes banked left in a swooping arch and flew off to the east from where they came.

By the time the sun truly began to set, a couple hours later, the lush green and tan farmlands had turned an ugly, reddish-brown or had even blackened. Cassy realized the enemy was targeting food supplies, not people. As if the EMP that destroyed food distribution wasn't enough, they were going after the food itself.

She sat in her lean-to with her chin on her knees, arms wrapped around her legs, and cried.

- **22** -

0800 HOURS - ZERO DAY +5

DURING THE NIGHT, Cassy had heard explosions to the west, which continued for an hour almost nonstop. The horizon had lit up in flashes. Each boom and thump caused her to jump a little, and it took quite a while after they stopped before she calmed herself enough to finally slide into a fitful sleep.

In the morning, still exhausted, she had a difficult time convincing herself to get up. Adding to her building fatigue, a deep melancholy settled over her with a simultaneous rage she didn't know how to handle, all of which sapped her will. Eventually, she forced herself to get up and packed her things, all the while fighting an urge to scream.

After packing, she decided to travel south toward Concordville and Highway 1, then west to Birmingham and, finally, north. She was not very cautious as she walked, doing little to take cover and, in fact, barely noticing the things around her. It was all she could do to force herself to put one foot in front of the other, to just keep going.

The fields she passed through, after leaving the belt of woodlands she crossed yesterday, only made her more somber. The once-lush crops were hardly recognizable. Whatever had been growing in these fields was now a thick brown, slimy mush. She tried to avoid it, with little success. Once, her shoes kicked up a blob of the brown goo that landed on her hand; she wiped it away, but it left a faint rash that itched even from so short a contact with her skin.

She also passed the burnt ruins of buildings, mostly grain silos, which were now twisted slag from which wisps of smoke still issued. No food would be found here, nor for miles.

She tried not to think of how many people died beneath those missiles, or from the defoliant spray itself. If it still burnt and itched now, what must it have done to those farmers it landed on? She shuddered and put the thought away, silently vowing to kill any of those invading bastards she came across, yet knowing she was powerless to actually do anything about it even if she did find the enemy.

She stopped when Highway 1 came into view, with Concordville just to the west. There was no noise at all from the town, and fear replaced Cassy's mental fog. She crept towards the town under cover of the greenbelt that bordered the highway, but soon wished she hadn't. As she approached the town, she saw smoke from numerous houses that had caught fire and were still smoldering.

Worse, she saw bodies littering the roads in town. Not dead bodies, she amended when she saw most still moved. Horrified, she realized they would be dead soon. Townspeople crawled along the sidewalks and in the roads, and now she could hear their cries of pain as they called out to one another. Not only could they barely crawl, but they also seemed mostly blind as well. They waved their hands in front of them and bumped into the buildings, the cars, and each other.

Cassy saw that the buildings had a dull brown tint. God

be merciful, she thought, the defoliant must have drifted over the little village last night and the tragedy unfolding in front of her was the result. She was thankful she hadn't fallen in the fields she had passed through, the deadly fields, but her relief was quickly replaced by a sense of guilt; she told herself it was only survivor's guilt and she would get over it. It was yet another thing to stuff into the box of pain and shame she carried inside her heart.

Tears came to Cassy's eyes, but there was nothing she could do for the dying. She stared at the scene for over an hour, crying all the while, desperately considering one plan after another to try to help some of them, but she could think of nothing. No, these Americans were soon to be casualties of war, and there was not a goddamn thing she could do about it.

It was time to cowboy up, she told herself. She was out of time for grieving, and now it was time to again focus on getting to her kids and her mom. She had to get them away from all this. Somewhere, somehow, she swore she would find them and get them to the farm. If it hadn't been sprayed...

* * *

Ethan sat at his computer and pressed the satphone's power button. He waited patiently while it booted up and connected with a "weather satellite." As the phone's home screen popped up, the dialog box on his PC popped up as well and showed a couple of messages waiting for him.

> *ATTN: Dark Ryder. Require status update. 20s remain secure, for now. Pls reply.*
> *ATTN: Dark Ryder. Decode:*
23490-193487-1-9374598-39876. Ack.

> *ATTN: Compliance required. Duty calls, DR. 20s
activated. Decode prior and Ack.*

Ethan frowned and typed into the dialog box: *DR ack
receipt. Will decode and ack. Require cipher #.*

The response came immediately. *Ack. Cipher P-1776.
You couldn't figure that out?*

Ethan laughed. Of course they'd use that cipher. It was a
couple hundred years old, but would be nearly impossible to
break if intercepted, not without knowing the right key to use
for the cipher or weeks of effort. He pulled out a dusty book
—of which he also had a PDF on his satphone—for cipher
1776. Opening it to the right page, he knew by heart which
letter positions to use for sub-cipher "P".

He typed in the correct response, based on the code
numbers given, and text flooded the rogue dialog box.

*Dark Ryder. 20s activated level Alpha, auth code 942-A.
List of friendly and enemy asset movements coded into
prior .txt file, auto-updates. You must decipher and recode,
then transmit via HAM. Patriot groups waiting for the intel.
MOST URGENT. The transmission will put you at risk, so
recommend relocate local prior to broadcast, and pray
collateral dmg avoids installation. Est enemy response @
under half hour, likely aerial response. 80% likelihood
armed drones rather than planes, so you won't see them
coming.*

Goddammit, Ethan cursed to himself. The only freakin'
reason they would need him to risk exposure was if things
were way, way worse than they'd expected. Obviously, the
invaders were wiping the floor with Uncle Sam's finest, faster
than anyone thought possible in risk assessments, even with
hypothetical EMPs. And his HAMheads told him of entire

towns and cities getting bombed out, from Pennsylvania to New York.

He could only hope things weren't so bad in Orlando and Alaska, if rumors of invasions there were true. Which he thought likely. But for Ethan, here in this red-zone, things were definitely bad. Very bad. And about to get a lot worse.

He walked to the back of the bunker and drew aside a decorative curtain that showed a huge picture of a scene from his favorite online multiplayer game. Behind the curtain lay a brick wall. He touched one brick, then another, and finally a third brick, and the wall split down the middle and opened outward. Behind it lay another segment of the bunker. It was lined with high shelves stacked with radios, mines, solar panels, segments of antennae. Tons of random bullshit. He frowned. It would take him a couple of hours to find and assemble the components to complete his assignment.

* * *

Frank walked back from the makeshift latrine they'd dug. He stepped on a twig and Jaz, sitting by the coals of the morning's fire, jumped up and spun around, her eyes wide. Frank thought she looked like a startled deer. "Damn, Jaz, you sure have great reflexes. We should make *you* the scout and let Michael sleep solid for once."

Jaz blushed and smiled, embarrassed. "I'm sorry, I just... I'm on edge. I don't mean to be, like, scared about things."

Frank stepped forward and put a hand on her shoulder. "Jaz, don't you worry. We're all scared. But you're one of us now, right? We're safer with another set of eyes and another gun ready, and you're safer with a family to watch your back, a group to belong to. So don't ever be embarrassed about what scares you, and just know that we have your back."

Jaz nodded and sat back down with a smile, and Frank caught sight of Mary nearby nodding in approval. It was good that Jaz had been accepted, Frank mused, because they sure as hell really did need another body in their group watching over his family. Of course, that made Jaz family too now, and so she was another person for whom they would all expect him to be responsible.

A touch on his arm took him out of his thoughts, and he saw that Jed stood next to him. "Hey, Jed. What's up?" Frank asked with a slight smile as they stepped away from Jaz.

"I got a bone for you to gnaw on, Frank. See, me and Amber, we ain't doing real well right now, you know? I reckon the stress is getting to all of us. But she's the mother of my daughter, and I love her. I just ain't *in love* with her anymore, if you get me. I don't think she is, either. But we're all in this crap storm, so we stay together, thick or thin."

Frank nodded slowly. "Yeah... What's your point, Jed? Anything I can do, you know I will."

"Yeah, I know. That's why I'm talkin' to you about this. See, if'n I catch the golden bullet or something else happens to me, I need to know you'll take care of my family. Kaitlyn loves you like an uncle, and I need to you be that uncle for her. And she'll need her mommy, so I need to hear you say you'll do it."

"Yeah, Jed, no worries. You have my word that if anything happens to you, I'll take care of Kaitlyn and Amber the best I can. Same with all of us, here. I think things are getting a lot worse before they get better, so now all of us here, we're a clan, Jaz included. And the clan will survive even if one of us doesn't. I swear on the Bible, or a short stack of rocks, or all the gods in heaven that we'll get through this together or not at all."

Jed nodded and smiled. "That's right proper of you, Frank. I appreciate you for it." Then he wandered away.

Frank watched as Jed left, and thought to himself that it might be needful to have some sort of meeting to formalize this whole "clan" thing. But now wasn't the time. Right now they had to pack and get moving while they still could. The hungry must be coming, and he didn't mean for his family to be there when the mobs arrived.

* * *

They were making poor time, Jaz noted. The kids weren't used to walking so much, especially over rough ground, but that couldn't be avoided. Frank had decided to head west before cutting up north between Chesterbrook and King of Prussia, on up to I76, and then they'd go west toward Lancaster, either on or near the freeway.

On top of minding the kids—who were the sweetest little things ever, Jaz thought with an almost wistful smile—they had to carry a rifle each, bullets, and a backpack. The men even carried two packs, one over their chests. They sure were good peeps, even though they made her carry so much. Frank said they would need all this stuff, and Jaz believed him because Frank was sharp as a tack. And they were all nice to her, so she could do a lot worse than this group. She had done a lot worse only a few days before, she reminded herself, and shuddered at the thought of the attentions showed her by those rednecks she'd been with. Okay, sure, she wouldn't mind taking care of Frank, or Michael, or even Jed, if that's what they wanted. It was what all men seemed to want. But these guys were different, they were married and gave a shit about that. None of them looked at her like a beer-and-taco happy meal. Maybe Jed did sometimes, but that was okay; Jed was probably the cutest of the guys, even if he wasn't as smart as Frank. But she'd never move on him —she'd managed to get Amber to like her, but that would change in a minute if she thought Jaz was prowling for her man.

Jaz lost her train of thought and nearly stumbled, but Jed caught her arm in time. "Careful, little missy," he said in that so cute cowboy accent of his, and she smiled and thanked him.

Looking around, she saw that the ground had suddenly begun to rise up, which was why she'd stumbled. They must be coming up on a road, Highway 202 if she remembered right.

Michael stopped the group then and snuck off toward the road. Jaz took a small sip of water while they waited, earning a frown from Frank. He'd said he would tell them all when it was cool to drink so they didn't, like, use up all their water on day one. Fair enough. She put the bottle away.

* * *

Frank waited patiently while Michael scouted out the highway ahead of them. He held his rifle at the ready, as did the others, but after the earlier ambush, he knew they all hoped never to have to use guns again.

Michael returned in a few minutes, gliding almost ghost-like down the embankment toward the group. Frank slung his rifle as Michael approached him.

"So what did you see?" he asked as his eyes darted back and forth between the road and Michael.

"Well, I'll keep it simple. There's a lot of cars, all dead of course. Things are scattered all over so I'm sure the cars were picked over real good already. I don't think we'll find anything useful in there. But I didn't see any people, or at least, no live ones. Two dead guys on the road but they look like they killed each other in a knife fight. That's actually very common, Frank, so if you can avoid a knife fight, do it. Better to back up and live than be brave and die. The guys on the road didn't get that memo, I guess."

"Did you see what's on the other side of the road?"

"Sure did, Frank. It must be some dink town called Chesterbrook, if I remember the area right, but it looks pretty deserted. A few people were wandering around, but mostly one or two at a time. We should be safe enough if we skirt the town to get to I-76, which takes us the way that lady told you to go to get to that farm."

Frank nodded and waved at the group to move out.

* * *

As the sun rose, SSgt Taggart looked around the remains of his unit. The day before, he'd had thirty soldiers from both his own unit and another unit they'd met up with from some other base. Today, only four other soldiers and two Humvees remained, along with plenty of ammo and one light machine gun to back up their M4 rifles.

The sounds of Newark echoed around them, mostly scattered small arms fire, and a small explosion in the distance. But also, the roar of lethal jets flying in and out of enemy-held JFK Airport.

Traveling through Newark had been a nightmare. Hordes of hungry people thought the soldiers had surely come to deliver supplies, or rescue them. They tended to get unreasonable when told to back away, and more than once they'd had to repeat the earlier tragedy of firing on Americans. He'd never forget the sight of a woman carrying a baby, both mowed down by a single bullet from one of his men. She wore a look of surprise as she fell.

Such scenes added fuel to the burning hatred he felt for the bastards who were responsible for all this. The enemy. Every man and woman in his unit had wanted a piece of those assholes, and by God, they were going to get it. Or so the soldiers had thought.

They'd made an effort to get to the Hoboken area, where they were to find some way to the island. The last intel they received said the enemy hadn't yet broken out of New York City, but the devil knew what Taggart thought of "intel."

They'd made it to the east side of Newark, traveling through what looked like any other warzone he'd been in, except for the odd "20" spray painted here and there. Then they finally ran into the enemy. The firefight lasted only about ten minutes. His unit was taking some casualties, but the enemy was getting the worst of it. Taggart had known that once the enemy broke, he and his soldiers would slaughter every last fucking one of 'em. They never got that chance, though, because two jets came screaming in low and mean from the east and unleashed hell on his soldiers.

Probably two full residential blocks were leveled in a heartbeat, along with virtually all of his boys and girls. And God only knew how many terrified civilians ate fire and lead, but the presence of civilians hadn't been a factor to the enemy birds, not when American soldiers were there for the killing.

The four soldiers with him were all he'd been able to round up as he fled through the fire and the smoke with enemy soldiers surging after them. He and the four would have been killed too, he had no doubt, had not some Puerto Rican with neck tattoos led them to safety in a section of abandoned tunnels. The guy said his name was Chongo, and he was part of the resistance. That there was any resistance was news to Taggart, but welcome news. Chongo said there were a lot of resistance fighters, and they were organized. It seemed his little resistance movement was the reason the enemy only wandered around in squads or more, like the ones his own men had fought and died against.

Chongo also said the leadership was not what Taggart would expect. Wait here, he'd said, and a leader will come to brief and debrief. Chongo told him that when the leader arrived, Taggart shouldn't stare or look him in the eyes; he was a criminal, and the only help Taggart would get in Newark, so behave. Taggart agreed; the operational parameters had changed, and he and his remaining soldiers would change along with them.

The soldier next to him, a Spec by his rank insignia, interrupted Taggart's thoughts. "You know we don't stand a chance as long as they got the airport."

Taggart nodded. "True, son, not in any kind of meeting engagement. But we're a long way from having the assets to engage the enemy like that. We're doing something else, now."

"What's that, Sarge?"

Taggart, sitting on the floor of the tunnel with his back to one wall, let out a long sigh and rested his head against the wall. "We're going unconventional, and we'll use this so-called Resistance to do it. They'll be our scouts, guides and local diplomats after they get around to sending this leader guy to chat us up."

* * *

Peter Ixin sat just below the crest of a hill with three other scouts. They sat well away from him for fear of his anger, which still overflowed. First that bitch of a spy had killed one of his scouts and wounded him. Then, after the vet had stitched up his scalp and announced that he had only a mild concussion, he'd been ordered on bed rest for two days while they kept an eye on him for complications. Screw that, he had told them, he was damn well going back out after her. She'd seen their stockpile and had to be stopped.

But his supervisor, or commanding officer, had said another team of scouts would be sent after her within the hour. Well, that had only given ol' Peter a deadline to get the hell out of that semi-prison. As if a few stitches were worth two whole days of bed rest! What kind of man sat by while others did his job for him? Not where he came from, no sir.

So, Peter escaped through a window, grabbed a hidden set of gear and a horse, and tore off after the scouts. He figured he was maybe fifteen minutes behind them, which was no problem at all. But then, only five minutes out, he heard the roar of airplane engines.

And then everything changed.

The planes flew in pretty high up, and one launched missiles that struck in the distance, back at the farm compound. Three huge explosions. In a rage he realized they had leveled the place he'd called home for the last couple of years. He doubted many had survived, except of course the scouts, most of whom were always out scouting.

Three more missiles flew southward, and from the light of the explosions Peter reckoned they hit the stockpile. That bitch spy must have had a radio or something, some way of letting the invaders know.

Then the other two planes sprayed some kind of mist over fields that were full of crops ready for harvest. He had no idea what the spray was but figured it had to be Round Up, or something similar.

He decided to keep going, to at least get some good old fashioned revenge by scalping their spy. He caught up to the other scouts in minutes, because they had stopped to argue. Go back, keep going, they didn't know what to do. Fortunately, Peter outranked 'em all and gave them some sense. They didn't argue too much about his order to keep going.

They spent the night on that hill, out of the fields and

eating cold rations, but the sun came up and it was time to move on. The fields all around, once full of crops, were now a sick, dark brown, which only added to the cold rage burning in his gut.

No matter what happened to him or his scouts, that bitch was gonna pay, he promised himself as they mounted up. His people were probably mostly dead and the farms in ruins, but no matter what, he was going to get justice on that spy. It might be the last thing he did in this world, but he refused to let so many of his people die in vain. Never in vain...

- **23** -

1200 HOURS - ZERO DAY +5

GRANDMA MANDY LAUGHED with joy as Aidan came down from the attic with a mid-sized cardboard box, inside of which were a dozen MREs. "How did you find that, Aidan?"

The boy smiled and preened melodramatically. "I found 'em in some of mom's boxes," he declared. Brianna was so happy to see the food that she didn't even make fun of her younger brother's showing off.

Mandy nodded. "She must have left them by accident, bless her soul. If we stretch these out, it's another four days of food," she said still smiling broadly.

A scream outside interrupted their moment of joy. "Stay here, kids," Mandy said.

She crept toward the window facing the street, to which they'd taped newspaper to block the view from outside. One little flap could be raised from inside, to see out, and Mandy placed her eye to this after lifting the bit of paper.

In the street she saw a man with a backpack. Despite a severe limp and blood on his leg, he was doing his best to run. He turned to keep track of whoever was chasing him, and Mandy saw that the man with the backpack was her neighbor, the one who'd thrown his tire iron through his own car window on the first day without power.

Seconds later two other men ran into view and tackled him together. There was a brief struggle, then one of the other men stood up from the tangle with a bloody knife in his hand. Mandy's neighbor stopped moving. The other attacker stood and then roughly yanked the backpack off the fallen man. He and his knife-wielding partner walked away with grim faces and then were out of view. They left her neighbor dead in the street.

Mandy slowly put the flap of paper back in place, drew a deep breath, and stood. When she turned to face the kids, she wore a smile for their benefit, but happiness was the farthest from her mind.

- 24 -

1400 HOURS - ZERO DAY +5

MANDY LOOKED WITH approval at her grandkids and the assortment of things they'd gathered for their exodus. They had a tent, barely large enough to hold all three of them; four full blankets folded, rolled, and bound with thin rope; two backpacks (the kids'); and a duffel bag. In the bags were knives, MREs, water bottles, a fork for each, and a little hatchet. Mandy thought three days outside should be enough for Cassy to arrive, if she lived, which Mandy forced herself to believe was the case. They had enough food and water for about that much time. She didn't want to think about what they'd do after that.

Mandy felt that Cassy would have thought of a dozen more things they'd *need*, but by God's grace, she had done her best. She didn't know all the things Cassy knew, and remembered with regret teasing her daughter for spending time and money on "that prepper stuff." Cassy had once mentioned "the five Cs of seventy-two hours," but God bless it, she couldn't remember what they were. Cover, cutting, cordage... What were the last two? She gave up trying to remember, and let out a long sigh of frustration.

Mandy set a note on the mantle, addressed to Cassy, which explained where they were going. She ended it by writing, "Find us at the Fairy Stones," which was a reference to Cassy's childhood favorite spot to camp, about an hour's walk from the house.

Aidan, looking over the collection of gear, chimed in. "Grandma, what if we have to boil water? Mom says to boil water or you get beaver farts. I laughed, but she said you don't laugh if you get Gondoria."

"Giardia, dear. And no, you don't." Which reminded her of another of the five Cs, Containers. "Be a dear and go get Grandma's small cook pot, sweetie."

Brianna poked Aidan in the shoulder. "And how are we gonna boil water without a fire, butthead? Do you know how to start a fire?"

Mandy smiled. "Be nice, Bri. I have a couple BICs in my pocket, we'll be fine."

She was oddly pleased that she had thought of the fifth C, combustion, on her own. Cassy would have done it faster and better, but Mandy felt reassured to know they had Cassy's "five Cs" covered. Wisdom from the mouths of babes... Truly the Lord had blessed her.

Mandy gathered the kids after Aidan returned with the pot, and made them hold hands for a prayer. Brianna groaned playfully, and Mandy favored the child with a smile before beginning.

* * *

Ten minutes later, her grandkids were outside with backpacks on. Mandy had her duffel over one shoulder and the blankets on her back, using cordage as a makeshift backpack rig. She was terribly sad to be leaving the house, but it just wasn't safe anymore, if it ever really had been.

They hadn't seen any people outside in an hour or two, but she still planned to go *away* from the direction the murderous men had taken.

"Okay, who's ready to go camping?" The kids looked sad, she thought, but then again, she too was sad at leaving. "Okay kids, let's go. Follow Grandma."

They got only half a block away when the buzzing began. Aidan was the first to notice it. "Grandma, what's that noise?"

Mandy tilted her head and listened carefully until her older ears caught the sound. "It's an airplane..."

"It's three of 'em, Grandma, look," Brianna yelped, and pointed to the east.

Mandy looked and saw three dots over the horizon, growing larger. They were in formation. "Military planes."

Then one of the planes veered off and took position higher and to the relative left of the formation. Seconds later she saw why when huge fireballs rose into the sky, and then they were hit by the noise of the explosions. *Whump, whump, whump.*

Oh God, thought Mandy, they're *bombing the town.* Fear washed over her like a wave. These were not American fighters. "Lord be merciful! Kids, run back to the house. *Run, dammit!*"

* * *

Frank and his family were moving single-file down an alley on the eastern outskirts of Chesterbrook when they heard the jet engines. Damn, and more damn! "Take cover," Frank said, perhaps louder than he intended, and turned to make sure they were doing so.

"Inbound," exclaimed Michael, and he joined Frank in looking for cover.

Nearby was a dry culvert and Michael pointed it out to Frank, who nodded and herded the families towards it. "Move it, move it," he shouted, and they did. The family ran, Jed and Michael scooping up the two younger, slower children. The first to arrive half-dove into the large concrete opening.

Then he saw Jaz trip and fall while coming down the small earth embankment toward the culvert opening, but she got up immediately. She was okay, he saw, so he just kept running. When he reached the opening, Frank stood by the entrance until everyone else was in. He was the last to enter.

Seconds later, the ground shook and the dark interior of the culvert lit up like daytime as bombs exploded all around the surrounding neighborhood.

* * *

Ethan sat in his bunker, waiting. He set up a makeshift antenna, running cable high into a tree then running it to a directional radio relay box set up well away from his property. By the time he returned to the bunker, he was sweaty and out of breath. Some minutes later, he set up the program to transmit the most recent decoding of the text file he'd received from the "20s," which now broadcast in a repeating loop.

His contact had said the enemy response would take up to half an hour, but boy were they wrong. More wrong than the time he'd brought only twenty clan-mates to raid an enemy stronghold online, and they'd all been slaughtered when some "allies" turned out to be a sub-clan of the people they were raiding. Sadly, he'd probably never get to play that game again.

In any event, it had taken only 16 minutes for the first bombs to fall. He suspected they'd bomb the shit out of

Chesterbrook until the transmission stopped, which could take quite a while. He hoped most of the people in town were gone already, but he would deal with the guilt of that when the invaders were pushed off American soil. This was an invasion, and he told himself there was no way to fight back without endangering innocent people. At least they would die in the fight for freedom, rather than by starvation and looting. Or so he tried to convince himself, without much luck.

* * *

When the first wave of explosions subsided, Frank turned to his people. "We have to get out of here. We're on the outskirts of town, still, so we have to go further. Is everyone okay? Anyone hurt?"

Jaz, sitting on the floor of the culvert, looked up. Her voice sounded strained when she said, "I'm not okay, Frank. I think I, like, Jango'd my ankle when I fell."

"It looks sprained," Michael said, helpfully translating Jaz's words into English.

"Michael, do what you can to splint it. We move in five minutes. Michael and Jed, you'll help support her when we move out. Amber and Tiffany, you take the flanks and keep your eyes open. Mary, stay with the kids and keep 'em moving. I'll help with that, but I'm going to be distracted keeping track of everyone else."

All around him, the others nodded. Frank yet again cursed at himself for taking the lead. This wasn't the role he'd have chosen, but someone had to do it and Michael didn't have the temperament for it. Plus he was more useful up front, as their only trained scout. Dammit.

* * *

Mandy peered out through the lifted little flap of paper over the window and fought back tears. Her house, tucked away on a back lot, was undamaged, but two blocks away, the town was burning in the aftermath of huge explosions. No one could have survived those bombs, she decided, and muttered a prayer for the dead, even though the preacher said the dead were already winging their way to paradise or the lake of fire. Still, praying comforted her and made her feel a bit less helpless. There was power in the Blood, she mused, and a prayer couldn't hurt.

Those planes weren't done with the town, she decided. If they were bombing civilians, well, there were a lot of towns left to blow up, including *her* house. Sooner or later the enemy jets would come back for her house too. They had to get out.

"Get ready, kids. We have to run before those planes come back." She shifted the little .38 revolver in her pocket and again prayed, asking God to protect them.

And then they were out the door. She glanced left and saw a trickle of people fleeing in the direction of the place she had intended to camp. She'd seen what people were doing to each other on the street and muttered quick thanks that she hadn't taken the kids there earlier. They would have been in the path of those desperate refugees.

She led them in the opposite direction, to the east skirting the burning areas, and could only hope it was the right choice.

* * *

Ethan sat with his elbows on the desk, holding his head in his hands. The last plane had unloaded its bombs a minute ago, but his radio was still broadcasting. The enemy would be back and would keep pounding the poor town until they took out his antenna. They probably had soldiers en route as well.

One of his monitors blinked on. He had cameras set up around his property, which were safely in the bunker at the time of the EMP. He set them up afterward, working at night to avoid being seen. They were his only early warning system.

On the screen, he saw two men and a woman enter his house, and the men were half-carrying the girl. She wore a splint on her left foot. Well, they were on their own, he decided sadly. But then things changed, and quickly: four children, three more women, and another man entered the house. They crouched down against a wall, avoiding exposing themselves in the window. Ethan could see that one of the men helping the limping girl had blood half-covering his face. Probably a scalp wound, he decided.

He was arguing with himself on whether or not to go up to help them—there were children there, for God's sake— when the decision was made for him. Another monitor lit up, and he saw four uniformed soldiers, not American, stalking toward his house with rifles at the ready.

Odin's Beard, he cursed using his favorite in-game swear word. There was no way he could let the enemy find those people in his house. They'd label the place for later investigation, and would definitely find the hidden entrance to his bunker. Shit.

Ethan grabbed his M4 from the desk and strode purposefully towards the hatch that led to the tunnel into his house.

* * *

Jaz grimaced and was grateful for the support Jed provided. She spared a moment to look at his head, which was still bleeding. Jed had jumped and tackled her to the ground when the soldiers came at them while they crossed the street headed to this somewhat isolated house, and as a result, he'd been shot instead of her. Grazed, she amended, after examining Jed's head.

"Get ready," Michael said while peering out the window. He slid back to the floor and checked his rifle. "Weapons check, everyone."

Jaz didn't know how to do that, but Michael wasn't really paying attention anyway. Must be one of his 'Nam flashbacks, she thought. In his head he must be in Crapghanistan or something. At least he knew what he was doing.

"Find a window and prepare to engage," Michael said. He wasn't yelling, but Jaz suspected she could hear that steely, calm voice clearly even in the middle of a gunfight.

Jaz scooted her butt over so she had better access to the window and made room for Jed as well. She was having trouble thinking straight, and couldn't see right, only a dot like at the end of a tunnel. Everything else was shadows. Good thing Michael was doing his voice-carry-thing or she'd never hear him over her heart pounding in her ears.

Then Michael was counting to... three? Every other thought was gone. In three seconds, she'd live or die. Soldiers would live or die. The kids... She didn't want to think about that.

"Three!"

* * *

Ethan ran the tunnel in great strides. At the end, it rose vertically to two hatches within the house above, one on the bottom floor and one on the upper floor. He decided popping up in the middle of a big group of armed and scared parents was not ideal, so he continued up to the second floor. At the top he slid a bookshelf aside, revealing the upstairs bedroom to which the bookshelf faced. The room was empty.

He crawled to the window and slid it open slowly, then rose to a kneeling position that let him see through the window without sticking his barrel out. No sense turning the window frame into a visible target box before he was ready.

From downstairs he heard a staccato of gunfire, and outside, one of the four soldiers flopped over backwards. The other three dropped prone and returned fire, and the fight was on. The enemy soldiers were spread out, maybe thirty feet between each of them, and they laid on the fire. There was a cry of pain downstairs, and Ethan hoped it wasn't one of the kids. He took careful aim through his "scout" scope, mounted far forward on the rifle's upper receiver, and squeezed the trigger. *Pop, pop* said his rifle and his target answered by catching a round to both the chest and face then flopping forward.

Hurray for two-round bursts...

* * *

Frank saw Michael move to where Jed sat against the wall. Jed held his arm, and blood seeped down his sleeve and dripped onto the floor. Then Frank had no more time to watch, as bullets from the soldiers again peppered the house. Frank returned fire, ducked, returned fire again, and spared a thought for the shots that had come from upstairs. Apparently, someone else was up there shooting at the oncoming soldiers, and he was glad for the help but worried what would happen if they all survived this mess. Was the other gunman going to try to shoot them, too, for trespassing? Or would Frank find a new ally? Well, they'd just have to figure that out later. If they had a later.

* * *

Brianna was scared shitless. Grandma kept a brave face on for Aidan, but Brianna knew the danger they were in. She sensed it all around. For once, Aidan was silent and just followed Grandma Mandy, obeying every instruction without comment. Brianna loved the little butthead, but, like, he could be real annoying. And she wasn't too sure about Grandma's directions. She loved Grandma too, of course, but Mom knew way more than Grandma about this stuff, and Brianna felt like she'd soaked up more knowledge about survival than Grandma ever knew.

Brianna realized with alarm that Mandy was leading them toward a block of houses. There could be people there, probably desperate and scared, maybe with guns. Or, the planes could hit that next and if they were all among those houses when they got bombed, there would be nowhere to hide.

"Grandma," she said as a rising panic took hold, "we can't go that way."

"It's cover, dearie," replied Mandy without looking at her. Mandy's eyes were busy darting all over the place.

Brianna resisted the urge to cluck at Grandma with disapproval. "Mom says to go around residentials if the shit hits the fan, Grandma." Not entirely true, but it seemed the easiest way to get Mandy to listen to reason. Of course Brianna knew more than Grandma. Of course Grandma wouldn't listen to a thirteen-year-old, even one who clearly knew way more than old, frumpy Grandma.

Brianna was relieved when Grandma changed course without another word, leading them a bit south to go around the clusters of houses. Dammit, Brianna thought. If they were baking a turkey, Grandma should be in charge. Trying to survive this crap? Brianna all the way. Stupid adults never listen... Well, she'd figured out how to get Grandma to listen; just bring up Mom. Okay, duly noted.

* * *

Mandy ignored her granddaughter's profanity for the moment. The Lord knew they had more important things to worry about right now, and she had to admit that Brianna was probably right about what Cassy would say. She felt a surge of fear for her daughter, wherever Cassy might be, but pushed it away. Whatever happened to Cassy, she would want Mandy to save her kids and so by God, she would do so if she could.

They skirted the cluster of residential buildings, and there was an intermittent popping noise from within; people were shooting at one another in there. She was immediately glad she'd listened to Brianna because truly the Devil was running amok on Earth right now and turning people ugly.

Mandy was distracted from those thoughts when she saw that the terrain opened up. They were leaving the residential area's outskirts and entering fields with many scattered copses of trees. She supposed they should dart from cover to cover.

In the distance was a lone house, well away from anything or anyone else. Okay, she decided, they would head to that house. Perhaps the Lord was showing her a refuge from the chaos. Surely the planes wouldn't waste a bomb on one lonely house, and beyond that house lay woods and nature, not more houses. It would be a way out if they needed one.

"Come on, kids," she ordered as she changed direction.

* * *

Jaz couldn't stop glancing at Jed, in between rising up to pop off a shot with her rifle and ducking back down to reload. She wondered why she was so worried about him because, like, he was just some guy. She definitely recognized that look he gave her whenever he thought she and his wife weren't looking, but he was nice and never said anything that was, like, super improper. Men always looked at her like that because, well, she was hot. Usually, her looks brought the kind of attention she didn't want, like with the rednecks, but it was weirdly different with Jed.

Bang! She fired another round, thoughts torn between Jed and the dudes outside. She was relieved to see Michael slide over to Jed to examine the wound.

Bang! Another shot. She looked over and saw Michael wrapping a shirt around Jed's arm, and heard him say Jed was "good to go." Relieved, she refocused entirely on the approaching soldiers.

* * *

Ethan was frustrated. After that first shot, he couldn't get a clear line of sight on the three remaining soldiers because they were slinking along the ground, moving from cover to cover, staying low and slow. He caught a movement from the corner of his eye, the one not peering down the barrel through his scope. He glanced that way and felt his stomach drop. Goddamn if there wasn't another team of soldiers moving up from the tree line a hundred yards away or so. And worse, one had an RPG.

Ethan knew with cold certainty that he was not a good enough shot to hit a target in cover that far away. When they decided to fire that RPG, then his house, his home, would be blown up. In real life, there was no "respawn point." Dead was dead. Shit, he would have to fall back.

He glanced at the tube opening that led to safety. He could escape. Those men and women weren't his problem. Nor were those kids... Shit. Kids.

"Fuck me, time to go full-on Die Hard," he muttered, and bolted for the stairwell. He prayed the people down there wouldn't shoot his ass off before he could save 'em. Wouldn't that be just ironic.

* * *

Frank popped up and let off a round, just as a soldier raised his rifle to fire. He missed, but the soldier ducked down as the round struck the dirt just next to him. As Frank ducked down again to reload, return fire peppered the window next to him.

And then an unknown voice sounded out from the wall opposite him. "Hold fire, hold fire!"

Frank whipped his head toward the noise and saw a man with an M4 standing in an opening in the wall that hadn't been there seconds ago. M4... Not invader.

"Hold fire," shouted Frank, and saw that Michael had his rifle aimed at the newcomer, shaking from the effort of stopping his reflexive fire.

"Hold fire," repeated Michael as he stopped shaking.

The new man wore a green tee shirt with some sort of computer game logo on it and jeans. He hadn't shaved in a week or more. The man's eyes were wide with adrenaline as he said, "Rockets incoming! Come with me if you want to live!" Then he started waving frantically at them to come to him. "Fucking rockets, man!"

Frank nodded, and shouted, "Michael, Amber—get everyone out. Follow that man, but keep your guns handy."

Then Frank fired as rapidly as he could out the window, heedless of aim. He had to keep the soldiers down in cover while his folks got the hell out of Dodge. He kept at it until he saw Michael standing at the opening, shouting at him that they were through, and then Frank sprinted across the room and through the opening. On the other side, the stranger slid the hatch shut, and Frank realized it was a bookcase that slid aside.

As Frank began climbing down the ladder, he saw the stranger coming down last and closing some sort of secondary door overhead. As it closed with a meaty thunk, the light faded, but then actual, honest-to-god lights flickered on. The light revealed a tunnel that went some hundred yards, then turned out of sight.

* * *

Brianna followed Mandy and Aidan, and her feet started to hurt. They had walked quite a way across uneven ground, and her Sketchers just weren't up to the task. Still, she didn't want to complain. Mom wouldn't have complained. So, she walked on and said nothing about the growing aches in her feet.

Some time ago they heard what sounded like a real firefight, lots of shooting, and then an explosion. She saw that the house Grandma was heading toward was on fire, and a thick smoke column rose into the sky. Mandy had them all take cover, and they sat uncomfortably in some brushes to watch and wait.

Ahead of them, a small group of what had to be enemy soldiers—they weren't dressed like American soldiers—approached the burning house slowly, guns ready. They spent twenty minutes or so searching the area, but with the building in full burn mode they couldn't get inside. No one inside could still be alive, she thought, and the soldiers must have had the same thought because, after surrounding the building and waiting those long twenty minutes, there was the sound of a whistle and the whole group moved off to the north, back toward town.

"C'mon, Grandma. Time for Plan B. Where to now?"

Grandma Mandy didn't move and didn't reply for what seemed like minutes. Finally, she turned to look at Brianna and Aidan, and said, "The Lord has shown us this place. It is a refuge, so that we need fear no evil. Trust in the Lord, little ones. We will go to that burning house, and when we get there the Lord will provide. He will send a sign, that we will know His will for us."

What the hell? Grandma was losing her mind, Brianna decided. "Listen, Granny, I believe in God and all, but I think the building blowing up was a darn good sign, don't you? We need to move on and find somewhere safe. Those soldiers will prolly come back when the house isn't all kablooey. I don't think we should be there when they come back."

Mandy wore a peaceful-looking smile on her face, and Brianna would have thought Granny was taking her glaucoma "medicine" if her eyes weren't so clear and alert. "Brianna, we will stay only long enough to receive our sign, God's sign. We'll leave if we find nothing, okay? But for right now, the soldiers are gone and there's no danger. Had the house not been set afire, the soldiers would still be there, standing between us and the refuge God will give us."

Brianna stared at her grandmother, at a loss for words.

Mandy continued, "I know you think I'm being foolish, but the wisdom of the Lord is foolishness only to the unbeliever. No amount of evidence is enough to prove the Lord to those who refuse to see. We will go there now while it is still safe, and if we find a sign then you'll know, you'll see that the Lord is our shield and our rod."

"Whatever. Let's get this over with," replied Brianna with a dramatic roll of her eyes. Then she stood and stormed off towards the burning building, Mandy and Aidan following in her wake.

It took only a few minutes to cover most of the distance to the house, but Brianna wasn't at all reassured when they got closer. If anything, the building looked to be burning even worse than she'd thought.

She heard the low roar of jet engines. She was getting to know the sound by heart, adrenaline beginning even before her mind caught up to identify what she heard. Brianna turned to look and saw three planes streaking toward the town. The planes veered slightly and now headed straight toward the house. Their path would take the planes directly overhead, she realized. Brianna tried to scream a warning, but her throat closed in fear and only a croak escaped.

Mandy saw them too, however, and screamed. "We have to run! This way, kids." Then she ran as fast as her older legs would carry her, turning to the right to head slightly south of the house toward a line of trees on the far side.

Brianna realized they had to reach those trees before the planes reached them or they'd likely be strafed, or bombed. No one would live through *that*, and so she grabbed Aidan's hand and pulled him along, running as fast as Aidan's shorter legs would allow.

They made good time. They passed by the house, but a glance at the planes told Brianna they weren't going to make it to the trees. Jets go too fast, thought Brianna angrily. "Come on, Aidan," she screamed, but her little brother was already going as fast as he could. For a second, in her panic, she thought of letting go of him, of sprinting to the safety of the trees without him. But she knew even as the thought hit her that she would never leave her brother or her grandmother behind. All together, or none. And anyway, she probably wasn't fast enough to get there even without him.

And then, to her left a deep voice shouted. It took a

moment for the words to penetrate: "Over here, you damn civilians! Get the fuck over here or die."

Brianna looked and then stopped mid-stride, almost falling. The source of the voice a medium-sized rock seemingly stuck to a flat panel, which was raised up on one side. Her mind registered that it was a *door*, a hatch, leading downward.

Grandma Mandy reached the hatch, glanced at the kids, and after a moment's pause, she was through the opening. Brianna and Aidan were only a few steps behind, but behind her, the buzz of jet engines had increased to a shrill and terrifying roar. She could almost *feel* the planes behind her, getting ready to unleash death. She glanced over her shoulder and saw the planes streaking right towards her. She looked forward again, but just then her foot caught on a rock and she slammed face-first into the ground, knocking the wind out of her.

Aidan didn't realize she was down and kept running. As Brianna struggled to her feet, gasping for air, she saw with satisfaction that Aidan dove through the opening. He was safe.

Brianna put her head down and charged toward the opening, but it was hard to move with the wind knocked out of her. She felt as though she ran through mud or molasses. But at least Aidan was safe.

Behind her, she heard the mechanical thump of something detaching, bombs coming off the jets probably, but she couldn't make her damn legs go faster. She neared the hatch, staggering as she went, then heard a different thump as something heavy struck the ground behind her.

And then Aidan and Mandy both stuck their heads up into the hatch. *Nooo!* Fuck! Go back down! But she was almost there… God, she had to go faster, had to get through in time, or Aidan might get hit too. The last few feet. Almost there. She leapt into the air, intent on diving through the hatch. Please, Mister, close it in time whether I get there or not, she thought.

And then she was struck by a force unlike any she'd ever felt, a hammer bigger than she was, swatting her like a fly. Her dive transformed into simply being propelled like a leaf in the wind, arms and legs flailing in all directions. The door lid rose up in front of her, and she knew she was going to hit it. She closed her eyes.

Please God, let Aidan be safe.

And then she hit the hatch at a million miles an hour, and everything went dark. Her last thought was for her brother.

- 25 -

2000 HOURS - ZERO DAY +5

CASSY HAD TRAVELED for hours and was near exhaustion, but she was only a mile or two from her mother's house. She was close enough that she had no intention of camping out for another night.

In addition to being close enough to her family to taste it, she was pretty sure she was being stalked. She'd had a weird sense of foreboding since leaving the encounter with the marauders, or at least it had started a couple hours later and hadn't left since then. The feeling only grew stronger as the miles passed.

Normally, Cassy wasn't one to believe in that premonition nonsense. Who actually thought that crap was real? But despite her skepticism, she could not deny the growing sense of dread in her belly. And there were three times since leaving when she could have sworn she heard a horse whinny in the distance. Once could be coincidence, twice was a stretch, but three times? Knowing the marauders used horses? Nope, no sir, Cassy knew she had a tail.

She'd been on high alert since then, and the effort had drained her mentally and emotionally. For the tenth time in an hour, she cursed her stupidity at declining SERE training due to the cost. Search, Evasion, Resistance, Escape—that sounded like just what she needed, given her current situation.

Fortunately, both her spirits and her vitality were buoyed by the thought of finally getting to her mom's and seeing her kids again, so she redoubled her efforts. Put one foot in front of the other; just keep doing that, she told herself, and she'd be having hot cocoa with Brianna and Kipper Snacks with Aidan in no time at all. She allowed herself to smile at that thought, but only for a moment, and then she was all business again. No sense getting killed a mile from home because she couldn't keep her fool head on straight, right? Damn right.

A whiff of smoke caught her attention. Not wood smoke, this had the pungent nastiness of burning plastic and so on, like a house fire. She looked around as she walked, but with the light fading, she didn't see any source for it. Yet, as she walked onward towards Chesterbrook, the smell became a haze, and then the haze became a choking cloud. She yanked her only cotton bandana out of a cargo pocket and wrapped her mouth and nose with it, but that did little for her eyes. She had to slow down to see through tearing eyes, and began to move in an exhausting half-crouch to get fresher air lower down. It worked, sort of, but her lungs still ached and her eyes still watered.

Ten minutes later, she heard the sure sound of a horse whinnying. "Yeah, you bastards, they don't like fires, do they?" she asked her nameless pursuers, glad that at least they'd have a rougher time than she did if they intended to keep to their horses, and if they let the horses go then they'd be as slow as she was. Either way, it helped her cause.

She emerged from a tree line close to town, and stopped in her tracks. There ahead of her lay Chesterbrook, and the whole town, it seemed, was burning. She could see craters scattered all over the place. The town had been bombed into oblivion, she knew.

A moan came from a few yards ahead. Cassy rushed toward it, stolen rifle in hand. In a small clearing in an empty lot lay dozens of bodies. Most were blackened. They'd likely been hit while fleeing, by whichever bomb had made the nearest crater.

Then she saw movement and approached slowly. A man lay there without burns but with both legs blown away. What remained were ragged, bleeding stumps. An ER would have been hard-pressed to staunch that bleeding without serious surgery. The man would be dead very soon, Cassy realized.

"Water," he groaned, looking at Cassy with wide, pleading eyes. Although she knew it was a waste, she couldn't help herself. She bent over him and gave him a sip of her water, and then another.

"What happened here," she asked with new tears in her eyes.

"Bombing. Planes, they bombed us..." His eyes rolled upwards as he let out one last, ragged breath.

Cassy reached down to gently close his eyes, then continued on her way. As she went, she saw more bodies scattered here and there where they had been caught in the open as they fled.

Anger grew within her, pushing out fear and exhaustion alike. She walked faster, then faster still, then finally running. Her lungs ached and burned from breathing in the toxic, smoky air, but she didn't slow down. She had to get to her kids...

Cassy turned the corner onto her mother's street, still several blocks from the house. She hardly saw anything around her. Her kids... No one could survive this. No! Her family *had* to be alive. She had not come so far only to find them dead now.

Lost in thoughts of her kids, she trudged passed a once-blue minivan with tires aflame. Abruptly, she found herself flying through the air with intense heat on her back when the burning tires ignited the minivan's gas tank.

She landed ten feet away in a heap and her head smacked a buckled, cement driveway. A shard of the cement sliced her open from her chin to just above her ear, and the skin hung in a flap. She tried to put her right hand to the wound as she gasped for air, but her hand wouldn't move.

She was probably in shock, she realized, and looked down at her right arm in disbelief. A shard of metal stuck out of her shoulder at the joint, at least six inches protruding. Part of her mind told her to leave it in; she shouldn't pull it out in case it had cut an artery or something. But she couldn't make sense of her thoughts, which tumbled around in a jumble.

Still dazed, she noticed the faint dusk light fading faster than nature could account for. Damn it, she was losing consciousness. There was some fear about whether she had a concussion or an open head wound, or perhaps just a lot of blood loss, but she just didn't have the energy to fight her slide into unconsciousness.

Screw it. She just wanted to close her eyes for a minute. She needed sleep. That sounded so wonderful.

Something banged her ankle painfully. Irritated at the distraction, she opened one eye, but saw only the night sky. She thought she heard a voice, but it didn't make sense and she didn't care. She closed her eyes again.

The next time she opened her eyes, she felt a bit clearer in the mind. She looked to her shoulder and saw that the metal fragment was still there, but it was bound up with strips of cloth and stabilized with what looked like socks. She couldn't see out of her left eye, but felt the constriction of bandages there, too. And she heard the murmur of a low voice, as though she was underwater. She turned her head to the left to see, fighting through the pain that shot through her neck when she did so.

She saw a stranger there with his back to her. He was muscular and wore jeans and a polo shirt. He had an M4 rifle slung over his shoulder. In his hands were two poles, which she realized extended down on either side of her; she was tied to a makeshift travois with paracord binding her chest and ankles. Shit, someone had taken her.

Adrenaline pumped through her suddenly, knocking away some of her pain and confusion. Moving slowly to avoid being seen or heard, she reached up to the cord at her chest and pulled the loose end, and it unraveled easily. She didn't waste time wondering why her abductor hadn't tied her more securely. She slid slowly downward until her hands could reach the bow tied around her ankles, and undid that knot as well. Hot damn, she was free.

Cassy jumped off the stretcher wearing a triumphant grin and staggered away from the man.

"What the hell?" she heard behind her, but she didn't look back. Then, ten steps away, a tidal wave of dizziness swept her off her feet and she flopped over to the left, sliding to a stop in the dirt. Fierce pain shot through her right shoulder; probably more damage from the shard, she thought.

She rolled over onto her back and saw her abductor running up to her. She fumbled for her pistol with her left hand but found the in-the-waistband holster empty. With nothing else to fight with, she could only kick out at the man. "No," she screamed, "you can't take me. Get away from me!"

The man stopped and looked down at her from just outside her kicking range. "Cassandra," he said in a deep and pleasant voice. "I'm not here to harm you."

He put on a smile that looked so very good-natured and made no effort to approach her when she scooted backwards a few feet on her butt. "Cassandra, I'm here to help you. You're badly injured. If you struggle, you'll tear your shoulder open again and you might bleed out. My name is Michael, and I'm here to save your ass, girl. I swear you're safe with me."

It was then that she realized he had known her name and she reeled, but as the adrenaline faded the clouds in her mind gathered once again, and she slid into unconsciousness.

* * *

Cassy opened one eye and blinked hard against the bright electric lights. She forced herself to stay still, trying to think and to figure out just where she was. She was in a small room, lying on a hospital-style bed with metal railings on all sides. She had an IV in her arm, and a bag of clear fluid slowly dripped into the line. On her left hand, she wore a pulse monitor, the machine behind her beeping at a steady rate. She decided she wasn't in immediate danger. They wouldn't have done all that just to kill her off later, whoever "they" were. She tried to sit up but the pain in her right shoulder made her gasp.

She heard a sharp yelp to her left and turned her head to see. Her jaw dropped. Sitting in a chair in the far corner was Brianna, with a bandage around her head and a sling on her left arm.

Brianna stood, slapped a big red button on the wall next to her chair, and rushed to Cassy's side. "Mom, you're alive!"

"I thought you were dead," Cassy replied, tears coming to her eyes. "I saw the house, and it was..." her voice choked with emotion.

"Burnt? Yeah, the whole town is," Brianna said as she wrapped herself over Cassy in a big hug, and Cassy ignored the shooting pain this caused. "But we're safe, Mom. All of us!"

The door burst open, interrupting the reunion; Aidan and Mandy rushed into the room, full of smiles, and Aidan bounced with excitement. She hardly heard the clamor of voices crying out her name, saying they loved her. So many hugs and kisses, each of which made her shoulder hurt, but she didn't care at all.

Finally her mother, Mandy, said with joyful tears streaming down her cheeks, "Welcome home, Cassy. We're safe, all of us. And we've made some new friends with some new toys. That's how we found you."

Finally, then, Cassy wept with joy.

* * *

Peter watched through binoculars as his prey disappeared into a field, along with the man who had helped her. Damn the stranger, Peter and his scouts had almost caught up to the spy when she and the man just seemed to vanish. Peter spent hours searching the field for a trap door or hatch, a hidden tunnel, anything. His frustration nearly boiled over when he couldn't find it.

The tallest of his three scouts said, "Boss, she got away. We should go home, and see who lived through that. It's time to take care of our own."

Peter frowned but didn't lower his binoculars. "I will not leave. You can go if you want, Ron. Leave your supplies and half your bullets, if you go."

The other man, Ron, let out a long sigh. "Boss, I'm not gonna leave you. I don't think the others will, either. If you say finding that bitch is more important than going back, then you're the boss and we follow you whether I agree or not."

Peter nodded. Ron was a good man, and he'd just proven it again. "That spy killed one of our own, Ron, and sooner or later she'll pop her head up again. Maybe the invader's bombs killed more people than she did, but we can't get justice for the bombs. Here, today, we are in a position to get revenge for what *she* did. Ron, I just can't live in a world where there's no justice. We, our community, we need this. We need this sliver of justice to bring back to our people so they can see that the world hasn't totally gone mad. There's still rule of law, sometimes. There's *still a point to going on.*"

Ron nodded and went to check on dinner.

Peter simply kept looking at the field through his binoculars. "I'm coming for you and yours, woman," he muttered.

* * *

Cassy sat in the small medical room with her family and their new friends, eating real food for the first time in days. Ethan had cooked up quite a meal from his stores in several deep freezers, and little Aidan seemed to follow him everywhere asking questions about his firearms, various devices, and how he had electronics that work when no one else's did. Apparently feeding hungry kids makes them like you. The thought made her smile. While they ate, they talked about their current situation and what to do next. Mandy said, "The devil may have transformed the world, but I think that all of us here, we're the proof that good people still exist. God will take care of us if we let Him."

Cassy resisted the urge to roll her eyes. She believed in God, sort of, but was certain that any god would only help those who worked hard to help themselves. "Sure, Mom. But we don't know what He wants for us, so we have to make rational plans and trust Him to do what is needful for us." Cassy knew how to get her mother to see reason without insulting her beliefs.

Ethan said, "We can't stay here forever. I don't have enough food for all these people for more than a few months. But more importantly, my bunker isn't truly safe anymore. Eventually, the invaders will find it. I have something to tell you all. The bombing happened because of me. I was contacted by a group called "the 20s" and they convinced me to broadcast coded intelligence to help the Resistance. I'm not sure who the 20s are, really, but I believe they are on our side. The invaders got a fix on the signal and bombed the hell out of the town to stop the broadcast. Eventually, they'll scour the area to find the real source when they figure out the broadcast was on a relay, and when that happens, we can't be here."

Michael grinned at Cassy and said, "You got guts, and skills, Cassy. You made it out there on your own. I gather you aren't military, but I bet between the two of us we could get a lot of training done, and maybe spread some knowledge to the rest of the clan."

Cassy nodded. She'd heard them call the group a "clan" before, and didn't see a need to argue the point. "Well, as you all now know I have a decent-sized homestead north of Lancaster. There's a lot of dangerous miles between us and it, but there's room for the clan, and food. A lot of gear, too, like radios that I kept in Faraday cages. Only a couple rifles, though."

Ethan smiled at that. "Don't you worry about that, Cassy. I have a stockpile here. Aidan can help me inventory it, and then Michael and I can figure out who gets what based on his military experience.

Frank stood and cleared his throat. "I'd like to thank

Ethan for taking us in, first of all. He saved the lives of everyone here, and I trust him even if he did bring the bombing. He had no way of knowing that would be the result," he said, and Ethan did not correct him. "So, if the clan agrees, then my mission is to get everyone here to Cassy's farm, with as much gear as we can carry."

Amber added, "I'll help Ethan inventory things. I'm good at organizing."

Cassy thought Amber's attitude toward Ethan was more than friendly, but then, her husband Jed had spent most of his time away from the group. Maybe a problem there, but they weren't Cassy's problem. Not yet.

The door opened, and Cassy's jaw dropped. Standing in the doorway, Jaz looked at Cassy and waved, timidly. Jed was behind her, standing oddly close to her. Another puzzle piece, but she couldn't dwell on that right now. Her anger rose and her face flushed. Cassy tried to sit up, but the pain in her shoulder stopped her, so she glared at the young woman.

"This woman is a thief," Cassy announced loudly. "I challenge her right to be here, and I won't take a thief to my farm. Bitch."

Jaz didn't flinch though she did glance to Jed for reassurance. Then Jaz said, "Cassy, I am sorry I took your pack. I was scared and dumb. I've been through a lot since then, and I risked my own life to save Frank and his group from some pretty bad peeps. I've earned my place here, and I'll do my best to earn your trust again. Can't you just take it at face value?"

Cassy looked to Frank, who seemed like the most level-headed of the bunch and the leader of his group. "Is that true? Did Jasmine save your lives, at risk to herself?"

"She sure did, Cassy. I don't ask you to trust her on my word, but *we trust her*, and she's one of us."

Cassy noted the finality in his voice when he said that. Alright, fair enough. She trusted Frank, if not Jaz, and she'd let that be good enough for now. "Fine, Frank. You have good judgment. I'll keep my eyes on her, but for now I'll let it drop."

Aidan hopped up on the gurney Cassy lay on and sat by her feet. "Mom, does that mean we all get to go to the farm?" He sounded terribly excited. "We get to be part of the clan, too?"

Cassy smiled at her son and nodded. "Yes, Son, we do. And for right now we're safe, we have lots of gear here to make our journey easier, and we know where we're going. Things could be so much worse."

The rest of the night was spent in happy talk of earlier times, and eating more food than they'd had in nearly a week. Yes, Cassy thought, things really could be worse.

# # #

* * * * * * * * * * * * * * * * *

For a **SNEAK PEEK** of Book Two
in the Dark New World series,
please visit: **bit.ly/dnw2peek**

* * * * * * * * * * * * * * * * *

About the authors:

JJ Holden lives in a small cabin in the middle of nowhere. He spends his days studying the past, enjoying the present, and pondering the future.

Henry Gene Foster resides far away from the general population, waiting for the day his prepper skills will prove invaluable. In the meantime, he focuses on helping others discover that history does indeed repeat itself and that it's never too soon to prepare for the worst.

For updates, new release notifications, and exclusive content, be sure to sign up for **JJ Holden's Newsletter**:

bit.ly/jjholdennewsletter

Made in the USA
San Bernardino, CA
21 January 2019